Rise of the Tudors

Richard III and the Road to Bosworth Field

Betty Younis

ISBN: 1982068795
ISBN-13: 978-1982068790

To Bruno

of St. Denis

Chapter One

April 8, 1483

England was at peace.

The bloody battles of the long war between the Lancasters and the Yorks, two families both descended from the Plantagenet clan of Anjou, France, seemed to have ended with the coronation of Edward IV, in 1461.

Through Henry VI's claim to the throne, however, warfare flared again during Edward's reign until finally, in 1471, the kingdom was united under his rule.

*****

April 9, 1483

Catching a chill, Edward IV died unexpectedly.

*****

List of Main Characters

Richard, Duke of Gloucester

Brother of Edward IV, and his most trusted general.

Elizabeth Woodville

Wife of Edward IV, and previously married. Born of a minor noble, yet raised by her marriage to the throne, she and her family were much resented.

Lionel, Bishop of Salisbury

Elizabeth Woodville's brother and confidante.

Anthony Woodville, Earl Rivers

Another of Elizabeth Woodville's brothers.

Henry Stafford, Duke of Buckingham

Considered the most eloquent orator in England, and companion of Richard.

Edward V

Oldest of Edward IV and Elizabeth Woodville's two sons. Believed to have been murdered while being held in the Tower of London.

Small Richard

Youngest of Edward IV and Elizabeth Woodville's two sons. Also believed to have been murdered while imprisoned in the Tower.

Bishop John Jonson

A very minor bishop and bibliophile retired to the vicinity of Leicester.

Thomas de Grey

Fourth son of a minor and obscure knight. A former priest and likewise a bibliophile.

*****

Wednesday, April 30, 1583

Westminster Palace

Midnight

"Elizabeth. *Elizabeth. Shhhhh.*"

The urgent whisper was barely a breath of warm air upon her pillow. A hand covered her mouth and she opened her eyes in fear.

"Wake up, sister. There is news." Again the words struggled to rise to a whisper.

"Lionel?"

"Shhh. Quickly now."

Gathering her chemise about her, she stumbled to the wardrobe and pulled a kirtle from it, dropping it over her head and not bothering to call one of her maids for its back lacing. Instead, she grabbed a shawl from the foot of her bed and draped it round her shoulders. Her brother stood by the door and as she passed through to the main room of her suite, he pulled it quietly behind her, raising the hammer on the lock and releasing it slowly lest the clicking sound waken his nieces. Elizabeth's hair tumbled about her shoulders but she ignored it, focusing instead on the man who stood near the dying fire. When she approached, the stranger dropped to one knee and bowed his head silently. Lionel joined them.

"Esterfield, rise, we have no time." Lionel's voice was harsh and impatient.

The man struggled to his feet, fatigue evident in his every move. His cloak and boots were spattered with mud and he had no cap at all. Elizabeth could not contain herself.

"Is it my child Edward? Is it the king?" Her voice was panicked.

Save for the shadows cast by the glowing embers, the room was cloaked in blackness. The circle of light in which they stood could barely contain the three of them. Beyond its feeble arc was only darkness, deep, cold, and void of comfort.

Esterfield looked askance at Lionel who nodded for the messenger to continue.

"Madame, the road from Ludlow Castle has been blocked."

Elizabeth sucked in her breath.

"I *knew* it." She began to pace frantically. "Who is it? Who would deny my boy, our good King Edward V, his kingdom? And my husband barely in the grave!"

She wrung her hands and continued along the same line of thought.

"King Edward - dead since the 9th - the 9th mind you, of *this month*! - and they come for his son? My son? The rightful heir?"

The messenger made no attempt to lift the pall but remained silent, head bowed. Elizabeth words hissed forth.

"Is it Hastings? That runt. Or Buckingham?"

Lionel put his hand on her shoulder.

"Elizabeth," he said slowly, "'Tis none of them."

"Well then who?" she demanded. "Who would show such hubris? Such misplaced confidence?"

"'Tis Richard, your own brother-in-law," came his dark reply, "And we fear he wants the crown for himself."

*****

The tale was jagged and sharp, causing Elizabeth to stare in horror at Lionel and the messenger as they spilled it out into the darkened room.

"Edward - forgive me majesty, King Edward - left Ludlow Castle as planned," began the messenger. Lionel nodded. "As you know full well, his coronation has been set for May 4th, three days hence."

Elizabeth waited and Lionel took up the tale.

"Unbeknownst to us, Richard went forth to greet our new king, and as protector, ride with him into London."

"Pray, I see nothing sinister in that. He is the child's uncle!"

Lionel held his hand aloft.

"Elizabeth, there is no time. Please, *listen*!"

He continued straightaway.

"Richard came from the north, having been at his Yorkshire estate at the time of Edward IV's death. He arranged to meet the new king Edward at Stony Stratford."

Esterfield took up the tale.

"Oh, aye, the dark heart of that man. They did indeed meet, but our good Richard Duke of Gloucester cried foul, and proceeded to arrest King Edward's escort."

"What?" Elizabeth blanched. "That is ridiculous - treasonous! Edward is but a child - twelve years old! He needs his councilors!"

"No matter. Your brother Earl Rivers, Lord Richard Grey, Thomas Vaughan - all were accused of attempting to deny Richard his rights as protector and taken away."

"Where are they now?"

"We do not know, Majesty. And Gloucester meant harm, no doubt, for he closed the road between Stony Stratford and London so that no news of his vile actions might reach the king's supporters."

"Then how did you get through?" Elizabeth asked.

"I ran two miles to my brother's farm, and I am here now on his horse. Majesty, they will move quickly to reach London and to do so in surprise, for in that lies the success of their plan."

"Plan?"

"Of usurpation."

The word hung in the air like Damocles' sword.

Salisbury took his sister's hands.

"You understand what this means?"

Elizabeth pulled free and began pacing again holding her head with both hands. Suddenly she stopped.

"And my other son, small Richard?" She looked with alarm at a closed door which opened off the hall in which they now stood.

"He is safe – I have posted a man by his bedside."

Her eyes met those of her brother with a knowing look.

"Sanctuary."

He and Esterfield exchanged a glance and nodded in agreement.

"Aye, our thoughts exactly. But it must be done now, for once Gloucester or his men arrive, he will block your path to the Abbey."

"Lionel, get the children. You," she turned to Esterfield, "Wake my men, get what you may of my belongings and follow on. We cannot wait."

"Aye," Esterfield responded, "Quickly then. Gloucester and his men cannot be far behind me."

Elizabeth threw off her shawl and ran to the bedchamber, calling out to her girls.

"*Now*! Wake and dress! Hurry!"

Warned by their mother's tone, the girls tumbled from their beds without questioning and threw on their clothes. In a trice, the three of them joined Lionel and a tousle-haired, frightened boy.

"Mama?" he asked sleepily. "Is Edward back? Is he king?"

Elizabeth knelt beside her youngest boy, barely ten.

"Small Richard, you must be very brave. Do you know what sanctuary is?"

"Of course – 'tis where we hear mass."

She smiled and put her hand on his cheek.

"There is that, but there is another type. A very long time ago, Edward the Confessor declared the Abbey at Westminster to be a haven for all who entered through its portals. In a charter of holy writ, he wrote that none may be removed involuntarily from it."

"What kind of haven?"

"The Abbey is a holy place child, and its holiness blankets all who enter its hallowed chambers, rendering them holy as well. Should you commit a crime, or be suspected of treason, or are being chased by your debtors, you may find respite in the Abbey. As a chartered sanctuary of holiness, none may be forced from it - it will provide protection to all in need of God's grace."

Richard nodded slowly.

"And are we in need of it, Mama? Sanctuary?"

She kissed his forehead and rose.

"Aye, my son, we are. Now come, let us be off."

Lionel lit a lone, tiny candle and they half-ran half-walked through the darkened halls of Westminster Palace. Time and again, he zigged this way or turned unexpectedly the other. The stone walls were smooth beneath their hands as they groped their way through the semi-darkness.

"Uncle, there is a better way!" cried Richard, eager to show off his knowledge of Westminster Palace.

"Shhh, of course there is, but we cannot be seen."

On and on they went until finally, a wooden door clamped with iron supports barred their way.

"Is this it?" asked Elizabeth in a shaky voice.

Lionel nodded and she continued on, frightened yet determined.

"Take Richard first, and the girls and I will follow. Do not look back. Do you know the Abbey door on the other side?"

Lionel nodded.

"'Tis the small one near the buttress."

Elizabeth kissed his cheek and hugged her son.

"'Tis always left open. Now check for guards!"

Lionel pulled the heavy bolt back across the oaken panels of the door and opened it slowly. He disappeared into the outer darkness, returning a moment later.

"Gloucester has not yet arrived."

He took his nephew's hand and without a word they stepped into the darkness. Their running footsteps could be heard reverberating through the labyrinthine passage. After a moment, she turned to her daughters.

"Girls, do not hesitate. Cecily and Elizabeth, see to the smaller girls, and remember, should I fall, run on - do you understand?"

She hugged each of them and together they followed the disappearing echo of the steps before them. They had just emerged into the moonlit courtyard when a thundering sound froze Elizabeth's blood. Richard, the fiend of Gloucester must have realized that she would try for refuge in the Abbey. After all, had she not done it once before when danger threatened? Within moments there arose such a din rose that she could barely hear her own voice.

"Run!" she screamed.

What seemed a thousand leagues away she glimpsed the light of a candle - Lionel held it aloft to show the way. It danced and wavered and as the deafening clatter of horses drew nigh, the women hurled themselves over the threshold.

"Seize them!" But the harsh command went unheeded. Elizabeth stared out into the night at the angry, sweat-drenched face of the dark figure mounted high above her on a rearing charger. Just as their eyes locked Lionel slammed the heavy oaken door and threw the bolt. Elizabeth collapsed against an ancient stone wall clutching her heaving chest. But there was more to worry about than the chaos and shouting emanating from the far side of the massive door. A great pounding sound was now coming from another part of the Abbey.

"What is this?" Lionel spit out angrily. "They *know* this is sacred ground - they would not dare…"

"We must stop them!" Elizabeth was up and in a knot they hurried towards the ominous thudding. But as suddenly as it had begun, it stopped. Lionel held up his hand. A strange silence fell deep and heavy across the scene, more deadly than the shouting voices beyond the door. Then, a persistent scratching and grating filled the air. They moved closer. Closer yet.

Down a long narrow hallway men could be seen moving in and out of the wall.

"They have breached the Abbey!" Elizabeth screamed. "Richard - hide! Go with your sisters!"

But before they could be away a man stepped through the wall, and turned to them with a candle held to his face.

"Esterfield! You made it!" Lionel ran to him and without a word joined in the operation at hand. Esterfield moved to Elizabeth.

"Majesty," he bowed deeply, "We could not get your belongings through yon narrow door and besides, we were told that Gloucester was almost upon us. We ventured to breach this wall to accommodate your things. 'Tis on the far side of the Abbey's central courtyard, so Richard and his men will not have heard."

He saw her pale, shaken face.

"Majesty, you are safe. Small Richard is safe. The Abbey has you now."

Elizabeth crumbled to the floor raising her hands in the eternal gesture of open-palmed thanks.

"Sanctuary!"

Chapter Two

April 14, 1583

Fifteen Days Earlier

Spring was late this year, and the north breeze which ruffled Richard's hair was sharp and biting. He did not mind, though, for the parapet of Middleham Castle keep was his favorite early morning perch. From its vantage, he looked out over the dells of Yorkshire, the rolling hills cascading through the land creating ideal pasturage replete with valleys and wide-flowing streams and rivers.

It was his, this place, in his bones since childhood. He leaned on the wall and drank in the cool wind. Yes, he knew every inch of the castle and its surrounds. He knew its rhythms too, and without glancing down he knew that the distant shout below was from a guard, demanding that the fortified outer gates of the castle moat be thrown open wide. The creaking of the ancient doors reached his ears, and he smiled. Now the wains on the public side of the moat would begin to stir.

Now oxen heaved and grunted as they pulled their loads across the bridge and into the inner courtyards of the castle. Within a very short time a small market was established there, with each vendor plying his wares in a loud voice. Meats, spices, cheese, fruits, pheasants, wine, ale, bread, hay: everything necessary for the rationing of an army was offered, for he, Richard Plantagenet, Duke of Gloucester, brother of King Edward, was in residence with his courtiers and troops. There was money to be made and the locals knew it, aye, for the Duke fed his men well.

Richard watched it all unfold beneath him as he sipped a cup of warm ale. To anyone looking on, his position that morning high atop the keep was a simple metaphor for his position in the kingdom of England - far beyond and above the mundane, master of all, second to none save the king, his brother. As Duke of Gloucester, his estates extended as far as his eyes could see and beyond, stretching across the length and breadth of his brother's kingdom, a brother and kingdom, he well knew, was greatly beholden to him. Who else among Edward IV's men could boast of fifteen years of military leadership and prowess? Who else defended the northern borders of his brother's realm? Who else? He and only he. And he had been rewarded richly for his undying fealty. Richard Plantagenet, at thirty-one, seemed to have all that heart desired.

What else could a man possibly covet?

*****

Thus far the day had been ordinary. Coming down from the keep for mass, he had humbly mumbled along with the priest and hastily crossed himself before retiring to his chambers to be dressed for the hunt. A ten-point buck had been sighted on the far side of York, and Richard wanted to claim it for his own. His valet followed him and closed the door behind them. It was only then that Richard began to undress, only then that he had to admit to human frailty.

God, it seemed, had a sense of humor. He had blessed Richard ten-fold but as a private joke between the two of them he had done the unthinkable: he had created him lame.

"Careful, there!" He spoke curtly to his man.

"'Tis the shoulder again is it, my Lord?"

"Yes, you imbecile, what else would it be - perhaps you have not noticed in your ten years of service to me that my *shoulder* is not as it should be."

The man held his tongue, knowing the signs of ill-temper. Richard continued railing against his physique, speaking half to himself and half to his servant.

"'Tis lower than the other, I can barely hide it."

His man said nothing, having heard the diatribe many times.

"And in being so it distorts my body. Look here, my torso seems squat and disproportional to my arms, does it not?"

"No, my Lord, I believe you are mistaken. Your clothiers and I take great pains to adjust your wardrobe so that none may notice. Indeed, if I did not dress you I would think you no different than any other man!"

Richard seemed mollified. His servant mentally performed the sign of the cross over himself for the lie he had just uttered. A person would have to be blind not to see the deformation, and deaf not to have heard the gossip about it which filled the kingdom like water in a river.

"It has not impeded my prowess on the battlefield."

The valet continued his work as Richard rambled on.

"I am as good with a lance and a bow as any other man."

His valet nodded and stood back, surveying his master.

"'Tis very attractive you are, my Lord. Now, do not let the maids of the county see you, for they will swoon fair away they will."

Richard smiled in satisfaction. But the moment was cut short by a banging on his chamber door.

"What the..."

A guard burst into the room.

"My Lord," he began and paused to catch his breath. "You must come at once. A contingent of men has been spied coming this way."

"What kind of contingent?" Richard spoke even as his mind raced forward. There were always plenty of men - nobles and knights - unhappy with him and his dictates or jealous of his fortunes. The amount he cared about such matters was directly related to how much protection he had about him at the time: on a battlefield he cared mightily; in a fortified castle...less so. Nevertheless, it was wise to be prudent.

"Pull the gates and raise the bridge."

"Done, my Lord."

Richard looked through the window slit but heard rather than saw what the guard spoke of. A rumble of hooves rose on the air.

"Take stations and bring me my lance."

"Done."

As he opened the door and strode from his chamber the level of confusion in the hallway was low but rising. It was not just Richard who gauged danger by the amount of protection at hand. Women and children were walking, now racing, for the fortified walls of the keep, the most ancient and impregnable part of Middleham. Richard hurried, too, for he could hear shouts coming from the courtyard. As he opened the door, he understood why - chaos had dropped like fire from heaven upon the place. The vendors who earlier had been only too happy to serve him and his compatriots were now panicked, shut inside the walls with no means of escape. They had no desire to be embroiled in a battle whose outcome, in all likelihood, would otherwise have no effect whatsoever on their daily lives. Richard's men had been caught off-guard and now shouted and screamed at their servants for weapons and armor. The stable doors had been thrown open and groomsmen raced to get their masters mounts ready for battle: those beyond the moat might be coming in peace; then again...

Richard made his way through the melee to the crenellated wall which encircled the castle on the interior side of the moat. The ladders had been hurriedly slammed and locked against the ancient stone works and he climbed one now. As he crested the top and made way to the outer side, a guard stepped forward.

"They say they come in peace."

"They all say that."

"They say they have news from the king, news for your ears alone."

"They all say that, too."

Richard studied the scene on the opposite bank. Twenty mounted men jostled each other on the narrow road.

"Why do they not wear our good King Edward's livery, eh?"

The guard grinned.

"Exactly, my Lord. And watch this – "

He raised his voice and shouted at the mass before them.

"Who speaks for you?"

A chorus of "I do, I do" spilled out from the group.

"You see, Sire? They are a rabble."

"And an armed rabble at that, it seems."

"Aye, Sire. They have long bows and their quivers are full. 'Tis reason enough to leave the bridge up."

A group of three vendors crouched as they made their way along the wall to Richard, bowing and scraping in the process.

"Well?" The guard asked them.

"No, we do not recognize any of them," came their reply. "They are not from these parts."

Richard remained silent, assessing the situation.

"Are their bows drawn?"

The guard checked.

"No, but perhaps the ones in front are hiding what those behind are doing."

Without more ado, Richard stepped forward into full view and made eye contact with one amongst the contingent.

"You there!"

The man urged his horse forward and away from his comrades. He waited.

"Send your men away and we will let you enter."

The man turned back to his companions to discuss the matter. Finally, the unruly group turned and trotted away from Middleham towards York. Richard watched in satisfaction.

"Now," he spoke softly to the guard, "Have my archers take up their positions here and along the keep. Tell the horsemen to mount and stand ready."

As the man bowed, Richard added, "And have my horse and armor prepared and waiting."

He turned back and studied the man he had chosen. He was certain he did not know him. Why, then, was he here? As the sound of hoof beats became distant, he ordered the bridge lowered and the gates opened long enough to receive the stranger. Only when they were once again closed did he climb down the wall to see why his day had been thus disturbed.

*****

The hall was large and cold, rectangular. Along one long wall were windows; along the other a mantel large enough and high enough for four men. Each short wall had three doors. The stranger was not shown to a seat near the fire but rather to a bench near the door through which he had just entered. Two guards, pikes at hand, settled in under a window to keep him under surveillance. He did not have to wait long.

A door on the far end of the room opened and a man entered alone. The two soldiers snapped to attention and stayed that way. But the stranger barely noticed their change in stance. He was busy taking in the man who now walked towards him.

He was of average height and build, but there was something odd about his gait and his body. It took a second to realize that it was not his pace but rather the length of his arms that gave the appearance of an uneven walk - one was longer than the other. And his torso. Despite the fine cloth and clever tailoring of the riding gear he wore, it was evident that his body was somehow truncated in a manner not normal. The entire effect was that of a being having been turned, scrunched and folded in such a manner as to make a return to normalcy impossible.

As he moved closer, the stranger was struck by the intelligent blue eyes which did not flinch. Wary eyes which looked upon the world with a calculating mien. Indeed, the man's face was one entirely suffused with caution - it was written in the deep creases which ran from nose to mouth, in the furrowed brow and the thin pursed lips. It was a face devoid of kindness but not filled with evil. It was alert and intent, but upon what, well, only the mind behind it could say.

The stranger shifted his glance to the man's hair - brown with hints of childhood gold. It suffered from a miserably inept cut straight across the shoulders which only accentuated that which the man clearly wished to hide. Straight across the front, too, with no curl, no flourish of design as if the simple plainness were a deliberate ploy to focus the viewer on the man's face, not his body.

"I am Richard, Duke of Gloucester. Why are you here?"

Of course, thought the stranger - it could only be him. He had heard the rumors and the ditties sung in the public houses across the land but those discounted the intelligence of the man. Lame - yes. Stupid -no indeed.

Richard motioned the two guards away from the fire and invited his guest to warm himself there.

"I said, why are you here?"

Again, the same piercing intensity. It was remarkable that the good duke did not even care what his name was.

"I am..."

"*Why* are you here?"

He clearly did not care. The rumors of a vile temperament which matched his vile physique were obviously correct.

"I bring news, my Lord."

Richard sighed.

"Yes, I heard you and your colleagues screeching that very theme from the far side of my moat."

He leaned forward in his chair.

"Tell me why you are here or I shall accommodate you further still…in my dungeon."

"My Lord, I bring news from the king."

"God's liver! Say it! What greetings and news does my brother, your king, send me? Speak, you nit!"

The stranger gulped.

"Sire, the news is not from your brother."

Richard was up in an instant.

"On guard!" he roared. The soldiers ran towards them as Richard rose to his feet.

"My brother *is* the king! What is this nonsense? I shall have your head for this treasonable statement!"

The stranger dropped to his knees and bowed his head.

"Your brother is dead, my Lord. I bring news from our *new* king."

Richard fell clumsily back into his chair as if felled by arrow shot.

"What say ye?"

"Your brother has died, my Duke. King Edward V, his son, is now king."

The stranger briefly paused then lifted up head and shouted out, "The king is dead. Long live the king."

Richard did not join him. He sat there motionless, thunderstruck and silent in disbelief.

Chapter Three

So a child would become the King of England: the whole of the kingdom would be led by a mere boy. He, Richard, the mighty Duke of Gloucester, would be forced to swear fealty and life to one not yet free of his nursery maids and tutors and all the other paraphernalia which went with childhood. He must fight war and wage battles for a prince who knew nothing, *nothing!*, of politics and leadership and kingship, of strategy and tactics against one's enemies. It was impossible yet true.

He listened in incredulity as the messenger from the south unfolded the full tale.

His brother, as ever, had taken no care for his health. His bawdy conquests and never-ending desire for rich foods and wine had set him up for disaster. Unhealthy in the extreme, he had nevertheless continued a life of vigorous hunting and fishing and debauchery. According to the man with whom he now sat, such a life finally bore its fruit.

No one was certain what brought on the king's sudden illness, but he had been out in the weather in previous days - some said he was hunting, some said fishing, some simply admitted they did not know nor care, for the all important upshot was that when he *did* reappear, he had acquired a chill.

This was not unusual in itself, considering the king's lifestyle. But when the days passed and he was unable to shake the cough which had taken hold deeply in his chest, the gossip at Westminster turned to worry. And then, before anyone even had time to contemplate the possibility, he was gone. Dead! Queen Elizabeth had immediately sequestered herself in Westminster Palace and called for her son, the namesake of her husband, Edward, soon to crowned Edward V.

The heir apparent was presently at Ludlow Castle in the Welsh marches. From there his presence served as a symbolic reminder of the crown and its power, for brigandry infested the area like fleas on a dog. Whether or not the ploy had been successful in its purpose was questionable, but now it was critical to get the young king to London as quickly as possible. It would not do for the lawless raiders surrounding Ludlow to get wind of the prince's new status while he was thus so isolated.

As she dispatched men to fetch Edward, Elizabeth also gave thought to Richard, Duke of Gloucester, her brother-in-law. He was yet in the north, having spent the previous year subduing the Scots and restoring Berwick-upon-Tweed to the English crown. Without hesitation, she sent forth a small band to break the news to him immediately. This first contingent should be trusted servants, men whose dress and attitudes would attract no attention as they raced through the countryside. She had no desire to alert the kingdom of Edward's death until his heir was safely ensconced at Westminster.

The men had arrived in the north that very morning, hungry and exhausted. While they took their fill in the great dining hall, Richard continued to question Elizabeth's messenger.

"And Edward is now on his way to London, you say?"

"No, my Lord, for we have ridden day and night to reach you with the news - that was Queen Elizabeth's express command. It is my understanding that the prince," he corrected himself, "...the King, will not leave Ludlow Castle until a suitable escort for the journey can be assembled there."

Richard leaned back and stroked his chin, closing his eyes as he did so. After a moment, he opened them and continued his stark line of questioning.

"And our good Queen Elizabeth?"

"She remains at Westminster Palace to await the arrival of her son."

"What of Buckingham?"

"My Lord?" The man seemed uncertain.

"The Duke of Buckingham, man, Sir Henry Stafford. Where is he at the present time?"

"I do not know."

Richard rose.

"Go join your brethren in the dining hall."

With that he strode from the room without waiting for the man to bow or thank him.

What an extraordinary thing! Richard turned it over and over in his mind, replaying the man's word and manner time and again on a repeating loop. Without thinking he made his way for the second time that day to his favored perch on the keep's high wall. There, he looked out across the valley once more and considered what fate had wrought.

The kingdom, his brother's kingdom, now in the hands of a child. But how long could a child hope to hold on to it? England was full of men of noble birth, men with titles, arrogance and unbridled aspirations. He knew well their ilk, understood their thoughts and ways for he had spent his life in opposition to many of them, both on the battlefield and off. They had a callous disregard for the rightful inheritance of the monarchy, unless, of course, it should turn their way.

Was it coincidence that just that morning he had felt the restless stirrings which sometimes haunted his days and nights? He began to tick off his accomplishments and possessions but stopped himself mid-stream. Was it time to face something he had known for some time? He was a man with everything. Everything, save a crown. And now a mere child…

He rattled himself free of deep thoughts and strategic implications. The immediate future demanded quick action. He stepped back down the aged and worn stairs lightly. Reaching the lower levels of Middleham, he called for his war council.

Chapter Four

Elizabeth Woodville was a beautiful woman. In the fashion of the day, her high forehead was carefully accentuated and extended by a hairline shaved considerably back from its original position. Her brows were thinned in the same manner. The overall effect highlighted her wide-set eyes, her cupid's bow lips and heart-shaped face. Her alabaster complexion was the perfect complement to her auburn hair and eyes.

This morning, her hennin was perched at a forty-five degree angle on the back of her head, and she had carefully rolled the front of its veil away from her face so that she could focus on the work before her. The belt of her empress gown rode high above her waist, while the deep vee of its neckline revealed a finely embroidered kirtle beneath. Overall, the look was one of streamlined elegance, and even now, after twelve children and nineteen years of marriage to Edward, she seemed to float within an ethereal cloud of feminine beauty and charm.

But as her face was kind and lovely, so her chin gave a more realistic view of the woman beneath. It was small and determined, not a footnote to her other features; rather, it provided depth and definition to them. Taken altogether, her look was one of thoughtful intelligence which suited her perfectly. She was a bright, intuitive woman who did more than just sit by her husband's side. Her family relied upon her position in the kingdom to enhance their standing and her maneuverings to advance their various causes were legendary. But England saw no malice on her part in these machinations; they were seen as the work of a queen intent on securing her husband's throne. There were even those who said that Edward even encouraged the rise of the Woodvilles, for by raising them to the ranks of the nobility he created his own coterie of powerful men, men who owed nothing to anyone save him.

She was at her desk when the letter from Richard arrived. Sending a servant in search of Lionel she opened the paper and began reading.

"Is it from Richard? He has been notified? What does he say?" her brother asked as he entered her chambers. It had rained all day and he scuffed his shoes against the stone floor to rid them of mud as he spoke.

"Aye," Elizabeth gave one answer for all three questions and motioned him to a nearby chair.

"He is on his way, he states, as soon as possible. He asks the whereabouts of Edward our new king, and says that if he has not already done so, he should not leave Ludlow without a suitable guard."

"Yes, yes, we all know this. What else?"

Elizabeth scanned the page.

"Condolences, allegiance to my son, sorrow on the king's passing…"

"What does he say about his own arrival here in London?"

She scanned the page again.

"He says nothing about that. Only that he sends this epistle immediately and more will follow."

Lionel opened the door and called for ale, bread and cheese. Declining to sit again, he stood by the fire warming his hands. It was a familiar pose of his, a habit since childhood. When faced with complex issues, he inevitably turned away from others as though to isolate himself in order to think. Elizabeth handed him the letter without a word and returned to her chair.

As the fourth son of an earl, Lionel had known from the beginning that the title had little chance of passing to him. The clergy was presented early on as his only choice and he accepted the training and the life without question. Secretly, he could not have been more pleased, for he was a scholar and a bibliophile by nature. Nothing brought more happiness to him than the acquisition a new manuscript. He did not cultivate relationships within the church as others did. For them, such contacts were a means of climbing ever higher. He found the practice distasteful in the extreme. He did not, however, pass the same judgment upon his own convention of cultivating great men who possessed even greater libraries. There was no service to large or small that he would not render one in such a fabulously fortuitous situation, and should that said noble acquire an extra copy of this or that precious manuscript and choose to pass it on to a most deserving clergyman, well, who was he to deny such happiness to anyone, especially himself? In turn, should he hear of a financially distressed noble on the continent, a fellow bibliophile strapped for coin, he would always alert his patrons to the opportunity. After, of course, he had perused the holdings for the benefit of his own collection.

When the day came and he was given an honorary degree from Oxford, he believed his happiness complete - he could mix with the dons and scholars there as one of them, no longer to be snubbed as a base outsider with a novice's penchant for learning. No, he became a full-blooded member of the club. When the church decided to anoint him Bishop of Salisbury, well, that was simply the currants in the scone.

A servant deposited a tray on a nearby table and Lionel joined Elizabeth there.

"What do you think?" she asked.

"I am not certain," he replied hesitantly. "On the one hand, he swears fealty to our new king. On the other, he declines to state when we might expect him here in London. He shows practical concern for Edward's safety, but again, asks pointedly where the prince is at the moment."

Elizabeth looked at Lionel thoughtfully.

"You think, perhaps, we should feel concern?"

"I do not know. Richard is your brother-in-law. He has been raised as I have, knowing that the title will not fall to him. I believe he is cautious, as any good general on the battlefield would be."

"Yes, I see that. He wants to get here quickly before he offers assistance, if it should be needed."

"Perhaps. But Richard also has blood that runs cold through his veins. Do not forget Henry VI…"

"That he killed him is not certain, Lionel."

Lionel shrugged and cocked his head.

"No, but he was there, Elizabeth. And he is cold and ruthless in his pursuit of what he wants."

"Or deems to be his," came her quiet reply. "And that brings us to the heart of the matter, does it not? Will our enemies see this as a chance to usurp the crown? Or, as they would put it, a chance to see the 'rightful' king upon the throne? And is one of our enemies mine own brother-in-law, my son's own uncle?"

A stillness settled over them. The Yorks and the Lancastrians, two distinct families of the great Plantagenet dynasty. Aye, but only one could rule the kingdom and each side saw theirs alone as legitimate. There was much to win but even more to lose in the battle which had waged between the two clans since St. Albans in 1455. But Edward had been a Yorksman, and the Woodville clan had accepted his cause as their own. The matter was not quite that simple, however, for Richard, the deceased king's brother, was obviously a Yorkist as well, one with as great a claim to the throne as his young nephew. And Richard was the antithesis of a Woodville supporter.

"Richard has never favored the rise of our family."

Lionel paced.

"That did not matter as long as your husband was on the throne, my dear."

"Do you think Richard would dare claim that he is more legitimate than Edward, my dead husband's own son?"

"How would he do so?"

Elizabeth thought, then shook her head.

"Richard is not a problem - I believe he will stand with us for he, too, is a Yorkist, a true Plantagenet. Besides, we are in a strong position. Edward's councilors are with him now - they will ride with him to London and protect him from whatever, if any, malfeasance might be planned. But I ask you this: who else would come for us should they get an opportunity, um? Who is *not* a Yorkist and bears watching?

"There are as many pretenders as stars in the heavens," was Lionel's wry reply. "However, there is one who bears watching above all others."

"That would be Henry. Pray he does not find out before our Edward is upon the throne."

"Aye, but there is another pressing matter as you well know, sister."

"The guardianship. Yes."

"His father wished Richard to be Lord Protector until Edward reaches his majority."

"Aye, but will he do so in a right and true manner? That is the question. He may be Lord Protector, but only with the help of Edward's truest councilors, my family, should he be allowed to guide the king. That is the only way that the kingdom will not be torn asunder once more."

They sat in silence, wondering what lay in store.

"Really, the next few weeks cannot pass quickly enough, my brother. We must needs put all of this to rest."

"Again." Lionel added. "I will write to Richard today and ask further about his plans."

"And I will inquire discreetly of Henry's current disposition."

Neither felt comfort, but then again, there was no whiff of desperation or intrigue in the air as might be expected at a time of such great uncertainty.

A quick bow and Elizabeth was once again alone. Her concentration was gone, replaced by a free-floating and nebulous fear of the future. Each time she tried to grasp it in order to examine it and thus be done with it, it melted away like fog on a wintry morn. She was held within its thick miasma. Without thought, she went quickly to her chapel and fell to her knees, praying for her family, for her son, and most of all, the strength to move through whatever was yet to come.

*****

True to his word, Richard acted swiftly. No sooner had he received a pledge of loyalty to the new king from his closest men and through them those of his troops than he set off southward. First was York, where again, fealty was promised by all. At each stage of his progress, he sent missives ahead of him to those he considered pivotal in the upcoming drama, for there would be drama regardless. Even if the change were smooth and seamless, the best of the available scenarios, there would still be ministers to appoint, Parliament to consult, and a myriad of other administrative responsibilities, which must be addressed sooner rather than later. Then there was the coronation, the public celebrations, the feasts - all required considerable planning and capital. But Richard knew full-well that those matters need not concern him. Others would see to such detail, and do a far better job of it than he ever could. No, he was occupied by a far weightier matter, and it was that issue which drove him from Middleham on the very day he received the news, led him to leave others behind in York to ensure fealty while he traveled on with a contingent of his most loyal troops.

Edward V was a child. His reign would initially be that of a minor. Accordingly, and in line with generations of tradition, a Lord Protector would have to be appointed to ensure Edward's, and the kingdom's future. And therein lay the problem.

A message had arrived for him as he moved on from York, alerting him to what he already knew, that his brother had designated him as the boy's guardian. Apparently Edward envisioned a regent who would rule side by side with the boy king, guiding him. Perhaps ruling in his stead on occasion, for no child could understand the complexity that was England. That was fine, but he was certain that the boy's mother, the Queen Consort Elizabeth Woodville, would not see things in that light. More importantly, neither would her family. They would want a council with as much authority as that exercised by the Lord Protector. Only then would their own interests be best served.

The Woodvilles were a small, upstart clan, whose crowning achievement thus far in their sketchy heritage had been Elizabeth's marriage to Edward. Richard had to admit, however, that they had played their cards very well. Over the course of the union, they had managed to marry their kin to the heirs of the Earls of Kent and Essex; Lionel was now Bishop of Salisbury; why, they had even found the gall to marry a Woodville boy barely twenty to the octogenarian Duchess of Norfolk! And Lord Rivers now ran the treasury of the realm. In short, there was not a niche of government which did not have some member of her family in a highly placed position, a position of authority and therefore one of power. They would not take kindly to someone besides one of their own running the kingdom.

His mind circled back to what would likely be the Woodville goal in the coming months, namely, the legitimization of some yet-to-be-formed council of Elizabeth's relatives, perhaps chaired by Elizabeth herself, in order to control the boy, and thus the kingdom, a council equal in power to that of his own in the role of regent. And yet his brother

Edward's wishes had been clearly spelled out – Richard alone should lead.

That problem was not an easy one. He turned his attention instead to another inevitable complication, the heretical, bastard-claimant to the throne he knew would rise once the news of Edward's death became public.

Henry Tudor's claim to the kingship was, in Richard's opinion, less than that of a common beggar on the streets of London. He settled deeper into his saddle and turned his thoughts to the matter in earnest.

Margaret Beaufort's son, an exile all these years, would no doubt use the coming change to challenge the peaceful order and transition of the crown to Edward. He would certainly declare his own claim equal in weight and right to that of the boy.

Was it? No, but that would not stop him and his clan from attempting to secure the crown for themselves. Where was the bastard now, anyway? Still in Brittany? Overall, Richard decided, Henry Tudor was the easier of the two problems. The foreign prince who currently supported him, Francis II, was likely open to bribery, particularly if Richard were Lord Protector. Why not give Tudor up and earn the gratitude of Edward V? And, of course, of Richard.

Whatever and wherever Tudor was, he must be dealt with posthaste, that much was sure. It would not do for a rival claimant to wreak havoc in the early going, when England needed to see a steady and sure hand on the tiller of state.

He made a note to set someone to the task of Henry, whatever that might end up requiring - or costing.

A courier pulled even with him and handed him a note from his faithful Buckingham. He would wait for Richard in Northampton, where, he stated, they could discuss the matter of Edward V face to face.

Richard smiled to himself. He had already received news that Edward had left Ludlow under escort and would meet him in Northampton as well. The drama had already begun it seemed.

Chapter Five

Northampton was a mere dot on the road to London and all its denizens turned out for Richard's arrival. His standard - a white boar emblazoned on a red and blue background - bedecked the pennants his troops held aloft, and while the horses' and riders' livery was dusty, their attitude spoke of authority. Some 600 men accompanied Richard, and he rode at their head at a dignified pace. But even as they crested the hills which lay about Northampton and made their way down its single street, Richard felt concern.

Where were the king's troops? Indeed, where was the king? There seemed to be no activity that spoke of a royal presence. Nevertheless he rode on assured in his mind that nothing was amiss. Perhaps he was simply the first to arrive. As they pitched camp and the local vendors began the process of supplying them food and beverage, hay and whatnot, a figure appeared at his tent door.

"My Lord, there is a man here to see you."

"Ah, Buckingham no doubt."

"No, my Lord. He says he is the Earl Rivers."

For the second time that day, a slight concern crossed Richard's mind but as quickly as it appeared it evaporated. Rivers stood directly behind the man and Richard beckoned the Earl in.

"Rivers, welcome."

Small talk ensued. Ale was brought, and after several cups, the men spoke of business.

"Tell me, is Edward on his way?"

Rivers shook his head.

"No, he has already passed this way and is now at Stony Stratford."

For the third time, concern made itself known to Richard. This time, however, he did not wave it away.

"Oh aye? He did not wait to meet me as we had agreed?"

Rivers caught the surprised tone in Richard's voice.

"No, my Lord, for Northampton is too small to accommodate your retinue and the King's. It was thought best to move on to Stony Stratford so that all might be bedded and fed comfortably."

"And how large is the king's retinue?"

"Two thousand men accompany him, my Lord."

Richard almost choked on his ale.

"I expected a large escort, considering the environs of Ludlow Castle, but 'tis very large, do you not agree?"

Rivers remained silent. Richard finally resumed the conversation on a friendlier note.

"Let us talk of the coronation."

"'Tis approaching fast," Rivers returned once more to the ale provided by his host. "The fourth of May, as you know, and the Queen would like Edward in London no later than the first."

Rivers began to ramble on happily about the ritual of the coronation. So absorbed was he, in fact, that he did not notice the hooded look Richard's eyes now wore.

"Yes, yes. Well, you will stay for supper and for the night, will you not? We will ride to Stony Stratford together, tomorrow."

Rivers readily agreed. But even as they spoke the same man who had announced Rivers appeared again.

"Lord Buckingham is here."

Rivers started up.

"Why is Buckingham here?" he asked with a twitch.

"He is come to provide a welcome escort to the King's entry into London. Now, let us eat, for I am famished."

*****

"Two thousand! They mean no good, I tell you!"

Henry Stafford, Duke of Buckingham, was not the kingdom's most attractive nobleman. Fair-haired and full-faced, his mouth protruded slightly in order to cover his teeth, a trait remarked upon more than once. But while he was not England's most handsome, he *was* its most eloquent. He was at his most persuasive when he was upset and at this moment, he was very persuasive. The flat cap he normally wore had been thrown aside along with his embroidered cloak. The supper they had shared with Rivers was long past, and the entire encampment was asleep, save for the two. They spoke by low candlelight in hushed tones.

"Did you not hear me? Two thousand men they brought to escort the boy to London!"

Richard did not reply and Buckingham banged on through his diatribe by himself.

"The boy is a hostage who must be freed!"

When Richard still did not join in, he took a deep breath and changed the subject.

"The size of Edward's escort is not the news I bring you."

"Speak." Richard shifted in his chair.

"The King's Council has made a move."

Richard stood up.

"Yes?"

"They have passed a resolution which states that there will be no Lord Protector. Instead, you will serve as the chief man of a *Council*. They are calling it a *'Regency Council'*. This group, not you alone, will guide our young king. Richard, this cannot stand. Do you see that it is yet another mechanism by the vile Woodvilles to maintain the crown within their own greedy clutches? Edward cannot be guided by a council – he needs a protector who knows and understands our kingdom and its nobles."

Richard still said nothing but sank back in his chair. So this is how it would play out. Before the young king ever got to London Elizabeth Woodville's family had stabbed at the heart of his brother's wishes. It could only be greed which drove them, not kingdom nor king.

"Buckingham, you yourself are married to a Woodville, so I hardly think you are in a position…"

"I was forced, as you know, to marry beneath me. They are no better than a cunning troop of monkeys."

"What do you suggest we do?"

This was the opening Bucking ham had waited for.

"First, we must free Edward from his kidnappers."

"They are his family, his guardians," Richard replied mildly.

"Nevertheless, we must send a strong message to the kingdom. Send those who are with him away, and let us escort him ourselves into London. The realm loves you and they will be heartened by your presence at the side of their new monarch."

"Your plan is flawed I tell you - they are his kin."

Buckingham paced in a fury. After a moment, he stopped suddenly.

"So you find two thousand men to be an excessive escort?"

"Aye." Richard was not certain where his friend was going.

"As would any sane man. Which raises the question: if they are not to protect the boy king, why are they here? There can be only one reason."

Richard cocked his head and waited.

"They are here to capture you, Richard. If they are not here for Edward, that is the only rationale which accounts for such a strong force. We know they are maneuvering to have your protectorship reduced to a one among equals on a council. This fits with that - they will control you and until they do they will hold you."

For the first time that evening, Buckingham hit a nerve. Richard had not been able to settle in his mind on a reason which might cause such an army to be raised. It was true that Ludlow Castle lay in the lawless hinterlands, but a troop a fraction of that size would be adequate to ensure the lad's safe passage. But what if the Woodvilles were planning on ruling through the boy themselves? Then such a large force made sense: they would enter London with such might that their actions could not be questioned. Men would be cowed by such a display and the power of the throne, well, it would flow to him with the might of the sword behind him.

Richard thought suddenly of his own kin. What would happen to them should the Woodvilles be successful? What would happen to *him*? His link to the crown was through his brother. It would be easy enough for Edward's relatives to claim that their objective was peace. In that vein, no one in his family would be safe. Not Richard himself, and not his son.

Suddenly, a change he had perceived as merely dramatic had become intensely dangerous.

Buckingham was still talking when Richard rose.

"Go now," he commanded him, "and very quietly, send a contingent to guard the road between here and Stony Stratford."

Richard paused before adding, "…should I choose to move, I want no news of my plans getting ahead of me."

Buckingham smiled in spite of himself. With a bow he was gone.

*****

Richard sat alone. A mild headache early in the evening had become a vicious pain which extended to his left shoulder. He played with one of the rings he always wore, twisting it this way and that on his finger as he stared off into nothing. Anyone seeing him might have thought him to be in idle thought, but those close to him knew better. Slowly, carefully, and methodically he was turning Buckingham's news over in his mind.

A council rather than a protectorate. A council filled with the Queen's men, none of whom favored

Richard. How long before he was removed from the group on some pretext? How long before he was sent to the Tower? His relatives picked off one by one until finally, only Edward IV's direct line remained. Richard and his kin a small note in some future history of England – the bloodline that died at the hands of its enemy. And his family? His son – Edward? He was not close to the boy, but Edward was not just his heir. He was his only child. How long would it be before they dragged him into the fray?

If he did nothing, Richard knew they would come for him. Perhaps not immediately, but aye, they would come eventually. And perhaps it *would* be in the immediate future, for they had already declared his protectorship over the young king null and void. Such action could only portend disaster for him and his family.

Word of Edward's escort, two thousand strong, and now Buckingham's news of these dire changes...Richard stopped playing with his ring and leaned back in his chair. So they would move quickly, hoping he would not perceive the danger until it was too late. The council, the guard, what would their next move be? It was clear that unless he wanted to ride directly to the Tower and likely proceed from there to the executioner's block, he would have to counter their plans with his own.

First and foremost, he must secure the king, for whoever held the boy held the key to the coming struggle.

Without warning, Buckingham stepped back into his tent.

"'Tis arranged," he said.

"Then sit, man, and I will tell you my plan - we must move quickly for we are at risk of losing everything before the game has even begun."

They plotted till dawn. Confident in their strategy, they exited the tent and prepared for the coming events. Even as the tent flap closed behind Buckingham, Rivers could be seen half-walking, half-running in their direction. His face was red with anger and his fists were clenched.

"Richard, my man tells me you have blocked the road to Stony-Stratford!" Rivers began shouting as he approached.

Richard stopped and watched Rivers as he came on. He skidded to a halt inches from Richard and leaned into his face with fury.

"What is the meaning of this? Explain yourself."

His voice had a flattened, dead and dangerous tone even as it rose in anger.

"And how did you know that I had blocked the road, eh?"

Rivers' eyes narrowed as Richard continued.

"Perhaps you were sending a note to our new sovereign?"

Rivers screamed in his face.

"And if I was? What is that to you? I am Anthony Woodville, the *Earl Rivers*, and it is my duty as his councilor and I warn you…"

"You *warn* me? You *warn* Richard Duke of Gloucester, the king's legal protector, do you? You may not issue a threat against me, Rivers, nor may you threaten me yourself."

Rivers stood mouth agape - he had not seen it coming. Richard closed the gap between them and screamed in his face.

"Treason! 'Tis treason! Buckingham! Take this man away and lock him up, for he threatens our good king's protector."

Buckingham had been thorough in his execution of Richard's orders the previous evening. From nowhere appeared a guard of twenty men, and despite Earl Rivers shouts of protest and violent thrashing, he was taken away. Richard turned to Buckingham and spoke in a low tone.

"We are in it now, Buckingham. We must stick it or die."

A low shuffling sound came from behind him and he glanced about. From nowhere a knot of men had formed around them, some dressed, some still in nightshirts. An uneasy restlessness flowed through them, contorting their rank into wary stances. Those with lances clutched them tighter; those closest to Richard - those who had heard his words - cocked their heads in mistrustful concern. All waited in watchful silence. Richard turned slowly in a circle, making eye contact with each of them.

"The boy king, Edward, must be rescued." He spoke bluntly.

A deathly silence was their only response. Had it not been within living memory that the kingdom had been torn apart by words such as these? There had always been rumors of Richard's hubris, his ambition. He read their minds.

"Oh aye, you wonder of my motives, do you not? Here now, you' - he pointed to a nearby man, "- 'you think perhaps that I, the Duke of Gloucester, want the crown for myself, do you? Your mind hearkens back to Henry VI...and you wonder...you wonder."

The man so addressed looked down and shuffled uncomfortably. Richard turned his icy stare on the growing crowd.

"As do you all. But I will ask you. Who have we served all these years, eh? Me, Richard? No. Did we subdue Scotland for me? We did it for the king, my brother. And just ten days ago, did we not all stand together and pledge our fealty to our new king, the boy Edward? Aye, we did and you know it. And so why would I rush to secure him against his own relatives you ask."

He continued meeting their hard gazes with his own.

"Our new sovereign is a mere child, open to the influence of those nearest to him. My brother," he raised his sword as he invoked Edward IV's name, "...appointed me the new king's lord protector. He did not appoint a council, composed of useless men whose sole concern is their own skin. The Woodville's would sit upon the throne themselves if they could, and since they cannot, they have determined that the boy will sit for them as their puppet."

He took a deep breath.

"Do we want this? Do we want our kingdom troubled once again by crass usurpers with no true claim to England's kingship?"

Slowly, those around him began to shake their heads in agreement with his incendiary words.

"We are men of the battlefield, and we will do whatever it takes to secure for England her true and rightful king, will we not?"

Now a cheer rose up and filled the air.

"So gather yourselves. Buckingham and I ride forward with a contingent to greet our new Edward - those who remain here in Northampton, prepare for prisoners, for I shall send as many of the king's false guardians back to your good keep as I can."

Without bothering to look at them again, as though he knew they were with him now and the matter had been disposed of, he stalked away with far more confidence than he felt. His casual command of the situation - bringing his men to heel with a few inspirational sentences - would hardly suffice should the Woodvilles choose to challenge his authority. If his own men, the very souls who rode with him in dark and brutal battle, did not trust him or the situation, how much less so the kingdom at large? And Elizabeth, Edward's widow, she was no ordinary woman - no, she had demonstrated an uncanny (some might say unholy) ability to read and manipulate both men and circumstance. He could almost feel a dark spider's web of intrigue settling upon the land; he would have to be careful indeed to avoid entrapment in its silken strands. Without a word he mounted his steed and turned towards Stony-Stratford, where his nephew awaited his arrival.

Chapter Six

April 1485

They had come for him at Ludlow. Ludlow, high on its rocky throne overlooking the Teme, deep in the Welsh marches; the idyllic setting for a childhood - far removed from court intrigue and the whispered plans and schemes of enemies and friends alike, alone and away from all else. Large sections of the eleventh century castle lay in ruins, perfect for the children's games he loved and played with his age mates on the estate.

Today had begun no differently than all his others. A long stint with his tutors had finally given way to dinner and finally, the freedom of play. But as his team had stood on the crumbling embattlements that day, hurling taunts at the one who had lost and now stood below them, a storm cloud of dust and horses and men rose up in the east. Games ceased and all the children scrambled onto the ruins to watch and wait. Across the valley came the great troop like a plague of locust moving steadily over the landscape. The drawbridges were taken up, the children called, the men fitted and mounted on their steeds. Ludlow was glorious, but vulnerable, in its isolation, and only when a small contingent separated itself from the group and rode on did Ludlow Castle lower the gate, for the smaller group was led by the Earl Rivers, Edward's uncle.

Edward recognized him first, and ran almost over the bridge to greet him. They had a routine, he and Rivers, in which they would slap each other's hand as a greeting. But this time, as Rivers threw himself out of his heavy saddle, he did not run to greet Edward, but rather bowed on one knee. Only then did Edward notice that the men with him did the same.

"The king is dead. Long live the king!"

Rivers cry was echoed by the men behind him, taken up by those still farther away, their mighty chorus filling the valley. Edward the child had become Edward the king.

*****

May 31, 1485

Stony-Stratford

Edward fingered the button on his vest like a nun her rosary. It was a habitual motion, comforting, one which became more pronounced during times of boredom or anxiety. The men around him seemed not to notice. They prowled in restless uncertainty, fidgety and ready to be gone from this place, but unable to leave until the Anthony Woodville returned from Northampton. Edward watched them, sensing their preoccupation with River's return. But his sense of anxiety did not flow from them - it was his own. Ever since they had all bowed before him at Ludlow, he had experienced increasing bouts of angst. Each spasm brought new worries which washed in like the tide and left behind the debris of mounting concerns. He had not liked it that Rivers left him the previous day. He was yet uncertain of this kingship business, despite his mother's attempts to prepare him. He longed for her hug, her reassuring tone and kind eyes.

Where was Rivers? It had been anticipated that he would spend the night at Northampton, for surely Richard and he would have much to discuss. The arrival in London, the coronation, the guardianship - all these were matters that would take time to work out. But Rivers had said he would send back word of when to expect him the following day, yet no word came. They were to have left at daybreak, moving on for London. Instead, they now looked backwards towards Ludlow, eyes strained to catch a glimpse of the Earl. But he did not appear. Instead, mid-morning, Richard of Gloucester rode into camp accompanied by Buckingham and a troop of soldiers.

Edward knew Richard well, and ran to greet him. Behind him, he heard the tense whispers begin.

Richard threw himself from the saddle and kneeled before Edward.

"My King."

Edward tried but could not stick to royal protocol - instead, he ran and hugged his uncle tightly. His uncle was here - all would be well. Richard closed his eyes and returned the emotion. After a moment, he stood.

"My king, we must speak in private." It was a good move on Richard's part - treating the child as an equal, as an adult. Edward puffed with pride at his uncle's recognition of his kingship, his manhood, and turned and looked at those who would follow them into the hall which had been set aside for the king's use.

"I wish to speak to my uncle, Richard, alone. I will call when we are done."

The men who were following in their footsteps were thick as winter fur. They moved en masse but stopped in a sulky huddle upon Edward's command. But they did not miss what the child could not see, the gleam in Richard's eye. Towards the back of the crowd, a young man spoke softly.

"Oh, aye, I have seen that look in many a man's eye."

The man nearest him whispered in agreement.

"'Tis the look of a man who, near power all his life, suddenly *has* power. 'Tis a dangerous man who feels it, knows it, but cannot have it."

As though sensing their words, Richard's eyes roamed the crowd attempting to see who whispered, who might not go easily. But nothing more was said, and the king and Richard turned and walked on.

*****

The equality disappeared with the closing of the door. Once alone with Edward, Richard reverted to the uncle-child relationship that had always been theirs.

"Your councilors must go, Edward. I fear they will wish to control you, to set your way as you ascend to the throne. 'Tis not good, boy - you must be allowed to rule and to come into your own without their interference."

They sat together but the conversation was not as Edward had expected. Nor was Richard happy.

"I do not agree."

What was this? The child does not agree with the man? Richard was stunned at how quickly, how utterly, Edward had absorbed his newfound power – his speech was infused with authority, an authority Richard found annoying in one so young. He had not counted on resistance, but rather, had assumed the child would respond as he always did – with childish enthusiasm and a lack of adult understanding. That was not the case, and as Edward continued telling rather than explaining his position to his uncle, Richard's agitation grew.

"First, they are not just my councilors, dear Richard."

Richard seethed. 'Dear Richard' – where had *that* come from, and surely he was not mistaken in hearing condescension in the words. Edward continued to educate him.

"As you know, they are my family, and they accompany me at my own command. Lord Richard Grey is my half-brother! And my chamberlain, Thomas, is always with me. So, no, they will stay with me, and I am certain I may rely upon their advice."

Richard smiled a hollow smile.

"But child, your father wished me to be Lord Protector. He named me above all others to see to your interests and those of your kingdom. Rivers, Grey and Thomas Vaughn – they have their own agenda. Why do you think they ride with such a huge number of men, eh? Two thousand when two hundred would surely do? Eh? My king, you are not their commander, you are their prisoner! They will show you off to the London crowds, then do as they wish regardless of your orders! Whoever heard of England being ruled by a 'council'?"

For the first time, Edward studied his uncle closely. He did not remember ever having seen the angst and anger now on display. Here, then, was the true man, the man accustomed to power in battle, the man accustomed to winning, the man who would be…what…a mere protector? He watched his uncle struggle to hide his feelings, and for the first time, Edward glimpsed the seduction of absolute power. For the first time, too, he understood its ability to sweep away his entire world. He felt the earth tremble beneath him, the shift exposing the thinness of their civil conduct.

"They are my councilors, uncle, and I do not wish them to leave my side."

Richard's response confirmed his newfound knowledge.

"They are under arrest, Edward, for they threatened the life of the Lord Protector."

Edward's face paled. He had come late to the game - Richard was moves ahead of him. What should he do? But even as he asked himself the question, the answer was provided.

"Buckingham and I shall escort you to London, my king. We shall see to your accommodation, your coronation, and your cabinet of councilors. Rest easy, sire."

As Richard spoke, a great sound rose from beyond the door - the sound of a mighty force of men turning away, leaving him alone with his uncle. A faint shout - was that Thomas? - echoed off the wall, but was drowned out by the thunder of hooves fading slowly, leaving the stage silent and empty save for Richard and Edward.

Edward bent his head to hide his tears of rage and fear. There was nothing to be done at this moment other than pretend to agreement and acquiesces to the circumstances. He needed time to think - the road to London regardless of his escort would provide just that.

Chapter Seven

He dreamt again of Tenby Harbor. Its fortified seawall, its clear blue, calm waters rolling deep in some unknown sway off the mighty ocean. Merchant ships from all the known world anchored in its bay, taking wool and cloth abroad and delivering olive oil, hemp, silver, and silk for England. Dotted along the quay smaller fishing boats and local skiffs tied to its moorings, each jauntily flashing its own vibrant scheme of colors. Ah, in his dream, he could feel and smell the place with its familiar scents and vistas. Most welcoming of all, however, was Tenby's language. How many years since he had heard English on the streets or in his home. As he walked along in his dream, each person he met spoke pointedly to him in his mother tongue, telling him of many things using words he had barely heard in his many years in exile.

But the dream always adhered to the same sequence of events. Eventually, the sun began to set upon the harbor and as darkness fell, his Uncle Jasper appeared from nowhere. Now suddenly a tense anxiety crept into the scene. They were running through the harbor town pursued by Edward IV's soldiers. They had come for him - they would kill him! – for whilst he, Henry, lived Edward could not rest easy upon the throne. The streets became narrow, the thunder of hooves behind them louder. He cried out to his uncle in fear. Without warning a ship appeared along the far distant end of the quay. Instinctively, he knew if they reached it they would be safe.

Again from nowhere a figure appeared between him and the ship. He could not discern the man's face but Jasper drug him onwards. Any moment his chest would burst in fear. But no – now the man stepped from the shadows. Thomas White! His friend! White beckoned them forward and as he did so a loud clanging filled his head as a gangplank was thrown down. They were across it in only seconds and in his dream, they were suddenly at sea. On the shore men hurled their weapons in his direction, bellowing his name in vain. But no matter. He was safe, and he would surely live to fight another day.

Henry always awoke at this precise moment in the dream. So familiar was he with it that he had come to study it over the years, wondering why, when so much of his life had been fraught with danger and mayhem, he always dreamt of Tenby.

He lay on his back now and once again considered it. Was it his way of reminding himself of the debt he owed to his uncle, Jasper? He almost chuckled aloud, for he had no need of a dream to remind him of that. Only his mother, Margaret

Beaufort, and his uncle had ever stood by him, ever rescued him when death seemed certain. Was it God's way of telling him that he was English and he should never forget that it was his brow upon which the crown of that mighty kingdom should rest? He sighed. Always the same ideas resulting in the same conclusion. If it had deeper meaning, its message was beyond his ability to grasp. In the end, all that could be said was that indeed, fourteen years ago, Thomas White, mayor of Tenby, had provided a ship to get him to safety in France. It was fortuitous that a storm had arisen and they had been forced ashore in Brittany where they had lived in exile ever since. As time had unfolded, so French loyalty to him had evaporated. Only in Brittany, it seemed, was he safe.

Henry put his arm under his head and glanced at the window in his bedchamber. The sun was coming up. Soon, he would dress and eat. He would hunt today, for the arrangement was that he should always ride in the forest in the mornings. Should his friends in England wish to send him a message, they knew he would be there each day. For all those years, a lifetime really, he had ridden out each day, hoping for something, anything, that would allow him to return to his true home. But thus far, the notes were only letters of encouragement, nothing more. Jasper had more patience than he, always reminding him that things take time to evolve and that in the end, all things pass. Initially, Henry had found it damn near impossible to temper his life to such an unbearably slow rhythm. But years in exile had quelled his rage against such unfairness and forced him to learn moderation in all things.

But even as he lay abed and played out in his mind how he would spend his time that day, a small dinghy was lowered from the side of a merchant ship anchored off a deserted part of the coast of Brittany. A messenger stepped in and the rowers immediately began fighting the choppy sea, making for shore. As Henry ate, the messenger paid the dorymen and waded through the shallows. Once on land, another man stepped forward to meet him with the reins of a mighty horse in his hands. Once more, the messenger paid before turning inland and galloping into the forest which abutted the shore. And as Henry stood in the graveled drive of home in exile, waiting for his mount and companions – they would have a lovely morning of it even with no news from home – the man dismounted and tethered the horse to a low hanging branch just beyond the gates of the castle which housed Henry. He patted his vest, reassuring himself that the purpose of his secret mission was still there. From a saddlebag he pulled bread, cheese and ale and settled down to wait.

On this day, Jasper would once again be proven right: all things come to an end.

*****

The boy had barely returned to his work in the stables before he heard the signal bell alert him that his services were needed at the castle's main entrance.

"What now," he grumbled. "How am I to manage my work here if they keep ringing for me out front, um?"

He grabbed his vest and hat - the lord was severe should his livery and colors not be worn when greeting guests. But as he ran and threw his arms into his vest in a single motion his stable mate appeared on the wide walkway that was the preferred path between the castle front and the stables. Behind him plodded the very horse he had handed off to Henry only moments earlier.

"What is this?" He asked his friend. "Did Lord Henry not want his usual horse? I just saw him off on his morning hunt!" A slight panic rose in the boy's voice, for it was never wise to frustrate or anger anyone above you.

"Settle down." His friend smiled at him and continued on towards the stable. The lad fell in with him.

"Well, then…what?"

"Aye, you would have had to have seen it. No sooner had the good lord and his companions left the drive for the forest than they reappeared at a gallop. No, not a gallop! An all-out rush, it was – a sight to see!"

"What happened?"

I do not know, but when Henry flung himself off his horse, he held a paper of some sort in one hand."

They walked in silence as they considered the situation.

"How long was he in the forest?"

"Um, not more than a quarter of an hour, for you see the chapel bell for early mass rang out as he galloped away, and the one signaling Joshua to take the sheep to the north meadow rather than the south had not yet rung. That would mean no more than half an hour, and I am positive it was much less."

"What do you suppose happened?"

"Well, you nit," his friend gave him a thumb flick on his head, "Obviously, someone was waiting for him in the forest and gave him the paper he had upon his return."

"Yes, I have heard rumors of secret messages being passed to him on his daily outings."

They said nothing more, but returned to their daily tasks. The intrigue would have to wait.

*****

Henry hurtled into the great hall where Jasper sat, playing at dice with his valet. Their table was near the great hearth at the far end of the room, and Henry did not stop running until he was upon them.

"You - pray leave if you please." He bent over, panting to catch his breath. His words were spoken in no uncertain terms to the valet, and Jasper rose as his servant left. He eyed Henry critically. His nephew was of medium height and on the slight side. He was always well put together in terms of appearance, which made his disheveled state alarming. The fact that his eyes were close to popping out of their sockets did not help.

"Sit."

Henry did as he was told, passing the paper in his hand to his uncle.

Jasper moved closer to the light of the fire and began reading.

"'Tis from your mother."

"As usual," Henry rolled his hand to indicate Jasper should read on quickly. After a moment, the older man let out a low whistle.

"So the king is dead!"

"Aye!"

"But I am not certain which piece of news is more vital, the one written upon the page, or the one left unspoken."

"I do not understand," Henry puzzled.

"Your mother states Buckingham is aligned with Richard of Gloucester."

"The king's own brother."

Henry's comment went unanswered as Jasper sat in thoughtful silence for a long moment.

"And then," Jasper spoke finally, pointing to a place on the page, "…she states that Buckingham sends you his regards. So the question is, why would Buckingham, the great and mighty Henry Stafford - *friend* of Richard of Gloucester - send you his regards? Eh? What is she not saying?"

Henry remained silent.

"Is he playing two sides? And where is Richard in all this? He is arrogant beyond belief. If his brother had lived, he surely would have been content with his role as England's leading Duke. But now…"

"Now the crown will pass to young Edward," said Henry. He gave a flourish as though bowing. "All hail the boy king, our newly minted Edward V."

Jasper laughed.

"Do not be a child, Henry. The crown will pass, aye, but a boy will not be able to hold it."

"Then who?"

Jasper looked at him in faith and fear.

"To the strongest." He drummed his fingers rapidly on his knew. "My god, there is much to be done."

He made to throw the note in the fire but on impulse tucked it securely within his vest instead.

"Does the messenger wait?"

"Of course. I told him it would be some time but that I would return with a message for him to take back to your mother. But what message do we send through her to Buckingham?"

Jasper cocked his head before continuing.

"And another question. How did Buckingham know of our communications with your mother? 'Tis strange. We must be careful."

Jasper patted him on the back as he left the room, calling out to him over his shoulder.

"Collect yourself, man, for your time has arrived. I will return shortly with writing materials so that we may begin to plan and alert our allies."

"My time has arrived?" Henry thought wryly as he watched Jasper hurry out. He wanted to believe, but as always, it was difficult for him to see any event in isolation. All things appeared to him as a linked chain of unending coincidence, fate, courage, character and raw luck. Perhaps this was just one more juncture which promised great things and mightily so, but delivered only ashes and ruin for himself and his would-be kingdom.

"My time has arrived."

How many before him had thought those very words, only to be taken down on some remote battlefield, or beheaded in some ghastly and hastily arranged execution?

And yet. If he did not at least try and rise, what then? A life of permanent exile in Brittany or some other foreign state, where the ruler promised sanctuary - oh yes! always! - and then traded him like a lifeless pawn upon a chess board.

He sighed and walked to the window. Yorks and Lancastrians. When had the dance begun, eh? And to think, each side wore a rose as its symbol of purity and purpose.

And now it was his turn. Henry Tudor's trial on the jousting field of English kingship. Well, he would have to, wouldn't he, for there was simply no other choice. Serendipitous coincidence or fate? He was about to discover which.

The door opened behind him but he did not turn. Jasper called out to him.

"Stop dreaming! We must get the message off before half the kingdom knows the tale."

Henry laughed.

"You think they do not by now? Then you know nothing of people, uncle, to say nothing of court life. But you are right. We should write immediately to our friends in England, with more to follow as we develop a plan."

He sat in front of the writing box supplied by Jasper. Opening it, he took out paper, quill, a blotter and a small pot of ink.

"So perhaps I will be king, hmm?" he said to no one in particular.

Jasper patted him on the back and echoed Henry's earlier sentiment.

"Let us hope, for otherwise what is left to us? An uncertain life in exile."

"If we are fortunate," rejoined Henry. "And if we are not..."

They sat together, and began composing.

Chapter Eight

June 1583

The old bishop rubbed his hands in delight.

"Ah, welcome, Thomas! I was beginning to think you had forgotten me!"

"Never!"

A merry smile lit the old man's face and he used his cane to nudge the chair opposite him in Thomas' direction. He pushed a warm cup of ale across the table to him.

"You looked chilled, and worn. Drink that and give me the news of the day before we begin our lesson."

Thomas threw back the drink and wiped his hand across his mouth. On the surface, the two men could not be more different. Upon meeting Bishop Jonson, most remarked upon his venerable age. He was a vision of flowing, snowy white hair and beard. His hands were gnarled and his back bent with the weight of the years, while his face was lined and cracked like a mirror dropped. He wore a black woolen cassock with a plain, simple sash at the waist. Most who had achieved such a vaulted station would be eager to wear the elegant garb the church allowed for its much esteemed leaders, and had he given it any thought at any time, Bishop Jonson might have as well. But he had not, for it meant no more to him than the passing of a cloud across the sky on a sunny day.

A closer inspection of the old bishop revealed kindly blue eyes and a twinkling smile beneath the wrinkled outer shell. But there was something else, and while most saw it few could articulate it: Bishop John Jonson was compassionate. His cats ate better than he did and more often; hapless insects which fluttered at the window in desperation were sure to be caught in a gentle hand and released outdoors; children knew he was a soft touch for molasses, jam and biscuits. He was beloved by all and with good reason. They might all be sinners, aye, but on behalf of the Almighty himself, the good father not only forgave, but sent them along with some cheery message or verse and perhaps a bit of ham or rye from his own larder.

Thomas de Grey was a good man as well, but Thomas was rough. The fourth son of a minor knight was his lot in life, and early on he had been dismissed by both parents as an unwanted mouth to feed. Surely his fate was to find some tenant position on an estate if he were lucky, or to beg in

London should it work out as usual for his type. But it had not. The three fates had looked upon him and determined that his life, his small, inconsequential life, would be different.

One bright, sunny day, thirty-five years earlier, Father Jonson had glanced up from his reading and seen a small boy, not more than five or six, working diligently at something in the dirt just beyond his window. He had thought nothing of it until two hours later, he noticed the child was still at it. In curiosity he went to out to inspect.

"What is your name, child?"

The tow-headed lad looked at him suspiciously with no answer. Jonson squatted and smiled.

"What is your name?"

"Thomas de Grey," came the childish lilt.

"And what are you doing, eh? Are you making lovely pictures in the dirt? Mud pies, perhaps?"

Thomas solemnly shook his head and stepped aside so that his work might be viewed. There in the dirt were the marks, 'tms bte'. Jonson stared at the letters for some time. How on earth had the child learned to write?

"'Tis interesting," he said and looked at the earnest face intent with purpose. "What does it mean?"

At this, Thomas perked up.

"Well, you see, father, those are *letters* and they mean words!"

"Where did you learn those letters, Thomas?"

The tiny face darkened.

"Your secret is safe with me," Jonson assured him.

"You read from the book each Sunday," he said simply. "I wanted to know how, too."

"And how did you learn?"

"Well, sir, you always leave the book open to the page from which you read and you always put a tiny mark by the verses you read. I, um, I um, um, I sometimes borrow the book, sir, and sit under your pulpit with it. I remember the words and the sounds and I teach myself their meaning. But I am always very careful and I always put it back."

"Good God. You mean you learned this on your own?"

Thomas smiled happily at the recognition and nodded.

"And I hear in the market, sir, I hear that there are other places with other books and when I get better I shall learn them, too!"

Jonson was dumbfounded. Thomas used his silence to point at his dirt work.

"You see, father, that says 'Thomas', and that says 'battie'.

"Battie?"

The child giggled.

"My pet frog - would you like to see him?" He began fishing deep in the pocket which graced the front of his dirty shift. Jonson stood.

"Come with me."

Thomas had followed on. Thus had begun his training for the priesthood and for scholarship. All because of a glance out the window by a compassionate human being.

As Thomas drained another cup of ale, the aged bishop rose and picked about some papers and books on his nearby desk. Returning to his chair, he smiled again and commenced.

"Now, lad, today..."

Thomas laughed.

"Father, I believe, after thirty-five years, we perhaps should move on from 'lad', eh?"

Jonson ignored him.

"We shall examine a bit of Greek which is not holy writ. I have chosen it because of the times we live in."

In a ponderous tone, he read aloud in Greek:

"When he, at length, despaired of life, he took off his ring and handed it to Perdiccas. His friends asked, 'To whom do you leave the kingdom?' And he replied, 'To the strongest.' This was how he died after twelve years and seven months."

Thomas ran his hand through his hair as Jonson continued in English.

"Who spoke those words, Thomas?"

"Alexander, of course. Alexander the Great said them upon his deathbed in Babylon."

The old bishop nodded.

"And I see why you would choose them for today's discussion," Thomas continued. He rose to pace.

"One hears strange things in the market these days."

Jonson nodded.

"Today, in fact, there is a terrible rumor abroad."

"That the dead king's own brother, Richard, would have the throne for himself?"

Thomas turned and looked at him sharply.

"So you have heard this, too?"

Jonson shook his head.

"No, but 'tis the way of the world, Thomas. You have been too long with your books and your God. You must be aware that not all in this world intend good."

"I do not believe it, sir," came Thomas' reply. "The child, Edward, why, no man would harm him."

Jonson drew a blanket across his knees before looking up at his friend. Thomas could read books better than anyone the bishop had ever known; his exegesis of difficult passages was frequently profound. He had a rough exterior and manner, completely at odds with his temperament and learning. Upon inspection, one would likely pronounce him a man of the world. And yet he could not read the intent or motive of even a simpleton, let alone a political master. He shook his head and sighed, wondering what would be his fate when the Father called him to heaven. Thomas sensed the old man's concern, patted his shoulder and sat, and they continued on with their lesson. After a bit, Agnes – the maid, cook, bursar and baker – appeared with bread and cheese. She was older, and had a face which spoke of hardship and angst. Thomas knew through rumor that the bishop had saved her, too, and that for that simple act of grace and kindness, Agnes had in turn devoted herself to the bishop's household and well-being. Those who might think to take advantage of the now elderly man were quickly sniffed out and turned away by the shrewd Agnes. If a tongue-lashing did not dissuade them, the large cane she kept close to hand always did.

Chapter Nine

May 4, 1483

May the fourth. The day of his coronation. His mother had promised him parades and jousts, feasts beyond number, holy blessings, an adoring public. Rivers, too, had assured him of his kingdom's rejoicing at his ascension to the English throne. All those who had traveled with him from Ludlow had paid homage to him, had called out his name a thousand times over as they bowed before him. The sun had been in his eye that day, the day he departed his cradle in the backlands of Wales.

He wore a cloak of ermine and gold and was mounted on his favorite black steed. It had been difficult to rein in his excitement or that of his horse. As one, like a kitten practicing its stalking maneuvers they had giddied sideways, the beast pawing the ground in reckless anticipation, Edward laughing and free, sure of whatever fate might bring. Together, he and his men - for they were "his" men now - had ridden in slow and somber state towards the crown which awaited him.

How long ago was that? He had not known then that eternity could be measured in days, but he knew it now.

Richard had sent all of "his" men away, replacing them with strangers who had answered to Richard in war and therefore did his bidding. They were northerners, men who had no knowledge of the boy king, and no wish to stand in Richard of Gloucester's way; men who saw the world through the lens of their own fortunes, and surely Richard was a better bet than a mere child who would not last anytime, for no child on a throne is secure.

And now he entered London, his capital. Now he saw the crowds come out to welcome him. But could they even see him? His massive steed had been replaced with a much smaller one, and beside him, on enormous destriers rode Buckingham and Richard, dwarfing him, hiding him, making him appear small and helpless. Before the entire entourage were wagon loads of weapons - four of them. He was told that these were proof that his Woodville relatives intended to rise against him for they had been cached just beyond London's outskirts. Edward, however, knew differently: his father had hidden them there should the Scots rise and rebellion reach the south.

He, Edward, had cooperated with Buckingham and Gloucester, had agreed to ride between them, for at the end of the day, he would see his family - his mother, his brother and all of his sisters. They would hold him close and help him fight the unknown evil he felt rising ever higher about him. His mother would know what to do.

In state, they rode through the streets and on to the Bishop's Palace at St. Paul's. Edward craned his neck to catch a glimpse ahead - surely any moment he would see them all, his mother, Cecily, Anne, small Richard.

"I say, where are my family? I do not see them yet?"

Richard said nothing and rode beside him in a still and silent manner.

"Uncle, did you not hear me? Where is my mother and my brother? My sisters?"

With a nod to Buckingham, Richard kicked his mount and trotted ahead. Edward looked at Buckingham, waiting.

"You see, sire..."

"No, I do not - *where are they*?"

Buckingham cleared his throat.

"They have taken sanctuary."

Silence.

"What did you say?"

"Sanctuary. Your mother and siblings have taken sanctuary in the hallowed chambers of Westminster."

"Why?"

His only answer was the cheering of the adoring crowd and a full silence from his companion.

They reached the palace, and with as little ceremony as possible, he was taken in to be safely housed and kept from harm. He tried not to cry or stumble.

*****

May 4, 1483

Thorney Island had long since disappeared. The small rivulets flowing round it had slowly silted up over centuries, filling in the contours and low areas until the island known even to the Romans became one with the city which sat across the way from it on the opposite bank of the mighty Thames River - London. The island's designation as holy ground reached at least as far into the distant past as the history of the Romans in England, and in Elizabeth Woodville's day, it was sacrilege to call it otherwise. Benedictine monks had first settled on Thorney, beating back the thorny undergrowth which gave it its name, and building in its place a small and primitive church. That church was not grand enough, however, for Edward the Confessor, and in its place he caused to rise the Abbey in which Elizabeth now had taken sanctuary.

Westminster rose and rose again, its gables and arches creating harmony and beauty as they reached out for heaven itself. Its towers and ramparts had seen centuries of English history unfold beneath their scarred and worn stones. And twice, they had kept Elizabeth Woodville from harm.

Elizabeth had always loved the place. There was light in the massive stones, in the stained glass of the windows, in the very pavements of the floor. The stillness of the place somehow carried grace across its wide spaces and gave her a sense of the eternal quest for beauty in spite of wars and famines, of clans and tribes and conflict and all the ugliness of strife. She had sheltered here for the birth of her first son, and now found herself once again taken refuge in its warm embrace.

But the Abbey was strangely empty now, for Richard had declared that no one might enter whilst she, Elizabeth, was locked within. She roamed the empty naves and apses, touching the pews as she walked the aisles of the long chapel. She prayed in isolated splendor at the great altar. But the deserted spaces served only to remind her of her own isolation - no kindly nod from God was forthcoming.

Today, she prayed for Edward, for within the scone she'd been given for breakfast had been a message. Such contact was deathly fraught, and she had skillfully tucked the note in a fold of her bodice before continuing on as though nothing had occurred. She laughed and spoke with the others, and was careful to follow her usual pattern lest her guards become suspicious. Only as she knelt alone at chapel had she carefully unrolled the scrap of paper and read it.

Edward would enter London today, accompanied by Richard and Buckingham. It was rumored, so the note went on, that Richard had deliberately planned their progress to pass before Westminster Abbey as a taunt to her. Did Edward know she had taken sanctuary? If so, did he know why? Previous messages, smuggled to her in various ways, had unfolded the terrifying story of Richard's interruption of Edward's triumphant march to London. Did the boy know of his horrifying resolve? Had anyone been able to reach him?

Her mind whirled and twisted and knotted in upon itself as it leapt from one idea to another as to how to aid the new king. This fiendish mental activity was a daily torture, and once again, she turned to her prayers in exhaustion. Perhaps God would help her son. Surely he would.

Some time later, she rose, determined to see her boy if possible. The circumstances were evil, but even a glimpse of his mother might encourage the child. She ascended the stone steps to the Abbey's high steeple. A narrow walkway - barely wide enough for one - encircled the gabled roof of the grand chapel and she made her way to the wall which fronted the street and looked out upon it. As if on cue a great commotion from the far reaches of the city made itself visible. Slowly, it ambled forward, closer and closer to where she stood. As the mighty procession turned and began to parade up the street below, she caught her breath. She had not bothered to put up her hair that morning and it blew across her face in the icy breeze of spring. She wore the dress she had worn the evening she had run to the Abbey and it clung stiffly to her thin frame now. Frantically, she searched the crowd beneath her.

Yes, there he was. Ooh, there was that vile Richard, riding with his henchman Buckingham. Little Edward was sandwiched in between them, dwarfed by their presence. They had mounted him on an inferior smaller steed and without a long look, one might not even see the child.

She stared at the retinue which followed behind the threesome. It seemed that everyone she knew was missing from the theatrics. She caught her breath involuntarily. Who would stand with her now? A small movement of her skirt drew her back to the moment, and she discovered small Richard clinging to it. He put his hand in hers and she looked out upon Edward, disappearing now in a wave of people and buildings, and she began to weep.

After a moment, she turned. There was nothing to be gained by maudlin sentiment. She needed a plan. Small Richard followed dutifully along behind her, trusting her always.

More and more, however, her thoughts jumbled into panic and depression. She squeezed the child's hand and stumbled on.

Chapter Ten

June 12, 1483

Richard lay flat on his stomach screaming in pain.

"But I have hardly begun, sire." The words were spoken in a droll and low voice in response. The man speaking continued to pour and rub a dark and breath-taking liquid across Richard's back. Each time more was put on, Richard clutched the table harder and howled in agony.

"Do you mock me?" Richard did not raise his head as he growled the words. He lay upon a long and low oak table with only a small throw across his buttocks to cover his nakedness. He clasped the table edges in pain and screeched again as more of the vile liquid was poured onto him.

This time, the masseuse turned questioningly to the physician behind him, who cleared his throat before speaking.

"Sir Richard, the man has only put the liniment on thus far. It stings as it works its way into your skin. Only then can he begin to massage your frame so that the pain in your shoulder might ease."

"What is in this potion of his?"

"Witch hazel, sire, lavender, certain oils and a special concoction I make in my own laboratory. I use it on a great many of my patients who have body aches and strains."

"The devil's own brew," Richard gasped.

The physician chuckled.

"Aye, all of my patients say thus. Some go so far as to say that I put it upon them not to aid in assuaging their pain, but to cause a greater pain so that they well nigh forget the first." He laughed at his own words.

The masseuse capped the bottle and spoke again.

"Now, sire, I will rub vigorously your shoulders and your back."

Richard focused hard on the candle which burned on a small side table nearby. Its flame flickered happily, flapping and curling to its own tune. The man leaned over him and rubbed gently at first. The burning sensation of the medicated oils passed, and as the man lengthened his strokes, Richard began to feel a lessening in the cramped ache of his shoulder. Again and again, the man rubbed down his back, relaxing him. Then clasping each shoulder firmly, he began to knead each one gently.

"Oh, aye, you are right, this treatment is far superior to others I have known."

The physician smiled appreciatively, watching over his aid's every move.

"Yes, I believe it is," he replied. "Now, sire, I shall instruct my man to knead a bit harder and more broadly across your entire shoulder. This should further relax the sickened area."

As he said it, Richard felt the man's hands begin working deftly across his entire higher back. Heavenly, he thought as he closed his eyes.

He was not sure how long the massage lasted for he began to doze under the fragrance of the oils and the kneading of his shoulders and back. The physician's voice eventually pulled him back.

"Now, give our Lord Protector his chemise."

The masseuse dipped his hands in a nearby bowl of water, wiped down Richard's back, and helped him rise as he dropped a nightshirt over him. The physician stood by the fire warming his night robe and as he stepped into it Richard felt the warmth penetrating even further into his bones.

"Oh, aye, 'tis the perfect finish it is." He murmured appreciatively as he sank into a chair pulled close to the hearth. "I will have more of this tomorrow."

The physician shook his head.

"'Tis not healthful two days in a row, sire. Your joints would complain, telling you they were overworked."

He warmed his hands before the fire.

"No, we will return in three days time, for by then you will be ready for another session."

The masseuse passed a warm glass of ale to Richard.

"Drink this before you sleep. You will sleep well if you do and be fit for the morrow."

Richard set the small cup aside.

"Fine, but bring me some ale now, and tell my servants to fetch Stafford. I wish to settle a matter before sleeping."

"Beg pardon, sire?"

"Henry Stafford, Duke of Buckingham. Now go."

The physician and his aide bowed and were almost out of the room when Richard shouted to them.

"And tell my valet to warm another robe like this one and bring it to me. I like the feel of the warmth."

As he waited, his brow furrowed and he closed his eyes, thinking back over the past few weeks and the disturbing news which had come his way, news which refused to die.

Since his entry into London with the boy king, as Edward now habitually referred to his nephew, there had been signs of trouble. He had proven adept at managing the various factions which questioned his increasingly powerful role as Lord Protector. Divide and conquer was his strategy, as though a battlefield lay before him. For those he could not intimidate, he awarded crown lands and titles. No matter that he did not have the authority. He had the crown seal and used it as he saw fit. Buckingham, of course, walked away with the lion's share of his newfound largesse - largesse at the expense of Edward.

And that, Richard had realized a scant two days previously, had triggered deep resentment among those who were not rewarded equally, regardless of the lesser role they had played in Richard's rise. Oh, the list went on and on: the Howards (of course - that clan was never satisfied!), Morton, the Bishop of Ely - there seemed to be no end. But those men were weak, and Richard knew intuitively he could cow them, bend them to his will. But there was one he could not.

Hastings. Lord William Hastings. He had stormed into Richard's chambers and demanded to know why Buckingham was being given what appeared to be half the crown lands! London, he assured Richard, and the nobility, could hardly stand by and let such an interloper weaken Edward V's crown – it was treasonous! Richard had listened courteously, made a vague promise about rewarding Hastings for bringing this to his attention (even though he, Richard, was the one who had rewarded Buckingham!), and sent him packing. Even with that promise, however, Hastings had departed in noticeable sullenness.

And then, insult to injury, news had come that the Woodvilles had been seen meeting with Hastings at his London home. And that moment, Richard had taken the little man more seriously. If Hastings should throw in his lot with Edward's relatives, Elizabeth's family, then his own plans would be severely threatened. There could be no reason for Hastings to convene with the Woodvilles unless a plot was being laid – a plot against him.

A soft knock on the door interrupted his thoughts and Buckingham appeared in a somewhat disheveled state.

"You woke me, Richard. 'Tis very late. What is the issue?"

Richard sneered at the whine and pointed to an empty chair.

"It seems Hastings is plotting against me and has seen fit to open a dialogue with the Woodvilles."

Buckingham yawned.

"I have news for you, sire. On any given day, half the kingdom is plotting against you. 'Tis not easy to be so near power which men covet for themselves."

Richard nodded.

"Yes, but Hastings is different. My men have seen him with the Woodvilles."

Again, Buckingham refused to rise to any level of excitement.

"He was the dead king's Lord Chamberlain. 'Tis natural he should gravitate towards that family. Besides, he is not known for an, shall we say, 'acute' intellect."

Richard became agitated.

"Do not forget, Henry, that you are almost as hated as I am. I have given you considerable lands and titles and you…"

Buckingham interrupted him with a hard look.

"I am not the Lord Protector, though, which is what they hate most about you. I have nothing to fear for I am not the one next to power, am I?

Besides, what would you do? You cannot punish half the kingdom for ill-considered or stupid plots against your person."

"No," came Richard's reply, "But I can punish one man, and if I punish him harshly enough, then the others are bound to take note, and rethink their treachery against me and the crown."

Buckingham weighed his words before replying.

"Then, Richard, I suggest you act with all haste, for if William Hastings is already meeting quite openly with Elizabeth Woodville's family - the king's own blood - then action, if intended, cannot be far behind."

For a long moment, Richard closed his eyes. This, then, was power? He reached for the drink left by his physician.

"Tomorrow, arrange a meeting with Hastings in my quarters at the Tower."

Buckingham sat up, suddenly alert.

"Just Hastings?"

Richard chuckled.

"Do not be stupid. He would never come alone. No, invite those you think may be sympathetic to his cause, those who can carry the word across the kingdom of how traitors to the crown are dealt with."

Buckingham rose and bowed, anxious to leave. Richard's order left him with a hollow sense of unease deep in his belly. He would do as commanded, for he had been enriched beyond his wildest dreams, but Hastings? To punish one so insignificant when so many were laying siege at the door?

"Oh, and Henry?"

"Sire?"

"Make certain the executioner is at the ready."

*****

June 13, 1483

Word flew through London like snowflakes on a blustery winter's day. Lord William Hastings, Baron Hastings, had been summarily dispatched that very morning. He had gone to meet the Lord Protector at the Tower...and had been executed. Executed! Reasons as to why were in short supply, but that Richard was behind it was definite.

A pall seemed to settle over the city. Those out about their daily business gathered in knots, whispering the news while casting furtive glances at passing strangers. They spoke of their children, not mentioning the child they were really wondering about; they spoke of Westminster Abbey with no mention of sanctuary; they spoke of king and kingdom and the upcoming coronation but no name escaped their lips. Some spoke of the incipient nature of evil, whispering that the smallest journey began with a single footstep. Then one more. Then another.

But no one dared give voice to the thoughts which occupied them all. Even as night fell and they were safely tucked away by their hearths with their families, no mention was made of what was happening. None at all, for what could they do? They were only small, inconsequential people after all.

*****

It was done, but the consequences were not as he intended.

Chapter Eleven

June 15, 1483

"No."

"Madame…"

"No."

"Mada…"

"Are you deaf? Do you not hear me? My husband was king, and my son will be king. God's liver! Why do you think you can address me thusly?"

Elizabeth had been told they were coming. Again. She had heard the stamp of a marched beat as they made their way through the sanctuary. And now, in this small apse she was to meet them. Again.

They had come to her routinely, repeatedly, over the past two days, always singing the same refrain.

Finally, she had decided she must have it out with them, regardless of the consequence to herself. She must shield him. The lead man spoke again.

"Madame, we do not come for ourselves, but on behalf of the Lord Protector, your good brother-in-law Richard of Gloucester."

"Oh, he is good now, is he? Pray tell, why has he not answered my concerns about my son Edward? Um? Why have my son's letters not been provided to me?"

"Perhaps he has written none, Madame. I hear he is busy indeed with tutors and with preparations for the coronation."

"Oh? Really? A twelve-year-old stripped of his natural family..."

"Really, my lady, such hyperbole is unwarranted. He is in the loving hands of his own uncle. How much more familial could his situation be?"

"And I hear just now he has been moved from St. Paul's to the Tower. Is this true?"

Silence was the only reply.

Elizabeth collapsed on a nearby chair.

"So 'tis true! My boy, our king, is being held as a prisoner in his own kingdom by his own uncle!" Her voice began to shake.

"No, Madame, I assure you, his circumstances are for his own safety. There is much talk about the land of insurrections and risings against our young Edward. Richard moved him to ensure his safety, not to imprison him. I assure you, Lady Elizabeth, that was the sole motivation!"

She looked him in the eye.

"Then *why*, pray tell, does our…" her voice turned sour, "…good Lord Protector, wish me to send my other son, small Richard, from our sanctuary here? Um? Answer me that, you knave! You have been duped by power, duped by Richard, duped by your own greed! Tell me, what has he promised you in return for delivering England's only other male heir to the crown safe unto his hands?"

A soft blush rose upon the man's face. Aye, this woman was what they said she was: sharp, intelligent, able to fence with anyone in a war of words. She had guessed correctly, for he had indeed been promised something wildly beyond his current means. But to attain his prize, he must deliver *Richard's* prize to him. He looked down, steeled himself and tried not to think of the child involved.

"Madame," he began softly, "Young Edward is lonely. He has no other children, no, not even his sisters, about him. You have locked them all away here in this holy place of sanctuary. Richard has assured you – repeatedly – of your safety and theirs should you leave the Abbey. You cannot believe him so devoid of humanity that he would cause harm to his own blood.

Edward has asked for his brother, small Richard. He does not sleep well at night and calls out in his sleep for him. Think of our king, my lady, and have compassion for him in your heart."

He could see that she was moved by this argument.

"Compassion for your child," he whispered, "…not hatred of your brother-in-law. Madame, let our future king be comforted by his only brother, not deprived of all company, of all playmates."

Elizabeth wept. Too much. Too much! She began pacing. Where were her champions? Her family? Was she the only one who saw what was happening?

He saw her waiver.

"Aye, my lady, I will tell you this. Richard of Gloucester believes you know of some threat to the crown, and that is why you refuse to let small Richard leave the sanctuary of our blessed Abbey. Believing this, he moved Edward to the Tower, for surely he must be in danger as well. He would be a fool not to! But if," here he hesitated as though taking her into his confidence, "…you should let small Richard leave this Abbey and go to comfort his brother, why, then, Richard would see that you have no danger in mind - that you *personally* know of no threat."

"*He* is the threat! *He* is the danger! Are you *blind*?"

The man ignored her outburst.

"And with that assurance, I would not be surprised if both boys were allowed to go where they will. Think of it, they could come here together - should you choose to stay on here. You could see them both whenever you liked."

Elizabeth turned her back on him and warmed her hands before the small hearth set deep in an old stone wall. A cold silence fell as Richard's man held his breath. After a moment, Elizabeth turned.

"Return this afternoon for my answer. But I warn you, sir, that should you arrive with troops and banners and swords, I shall not receive you. Do you understand?"

He bowed silently and backed from the room.

"Almost there," he thought to himself, "Almost there."

As his retinue exited the Abbey, a young man approached him on the front steps with a questioning look on his soft features.

"Tell the Lord Protector I believe I have found the secret to getting the boy. It shall not be long now."

The lad bowed and turning, began running towards Baynard's Castle.

*****

Elizabeth crossed herself repeatedly as she entered the main sanctuary of Westminster. She was alone. Light from the stained glass in the windows fractured and fell in shards on the floor around her. As she knelt at the altar and bowed her head before God, she prayed fervently, but the only response came from the deep silence of the place as it echoed against her soul. God's answer, it seemed, was for her to look inward. She placed her head on her hands and sobbed.

She did not know if Edward was lost unto her and his kingdom. No one did, for Richard kept news of the boy-king away from all but a chosen few. Richard's vile messenger had been right, though - despite being king, the child must be terrified, frightened at his situation and no doubt wondering why his own family had abandoned him. She had prepared Edward for many things: for leadership; for service to God, the crown and family; for compassion as the Savior demanded of all his disciples. But she had not prepared her little boy for this.

Two hours passed before she rose dry-eyed and clear-headed. A small room had been set aside for her use, and she went there now. From inside the quilt on the bed, she withdrew two scraps of paper on which news had been smuggled to her. Aware that she might one day need to send news in the other direction and unable to persuade her guards to provide her with paper, she had saved them for that purpose. Hoping that God would forgive her, she had purloined a pen and ink from the Bishop's chambers and now carefully fished them out of the batting. Unstopping the inkwell, she began to write.

As late afternoon approached, she made her way to the room in which her other children, small Richard and the girls, were saying mass. She waited patiently for the service to finish before taking her son in her arms with a gay smile.

"Small Richard, I have news of your brother!"

The boy smiled happily and she continued.

"He has requested your presence!"

A squeal of excitement escaped him.

"Now," his mother continued, "There are dangers abroad, and I expect the two of you to face them like the princes you are - strong and brave."

Richard nodded happily. An adventure!

"When will I see him?"

"Today, my son - imagine that!" She ran her hand over his curly hair.

"And," here she lowered her voice to a conspiratorial whisper, "...he asks that you bring him a message from me. But he commands that the message be kept from all - only the three of us shall know of it."

Richard puffed with pride and nodded solemnly.

"I have written on small bits of paper that I will hide about your person. Should you be asked, God and King demand that you pretend to know nothing. Can you do that for Edward and me, my son?"

Again small Richard nodded happily and Elizabeth began surreptitiously tucking paper within his pantaloons and his shoes.

"Tell no one," she whispered in his ear, "...Deny to all save your blessed brother."

Small Richard was delighted.

*****

As promised, the man returned alone. Surprise crossed his features as Elizabeth waved to him gaily and introduced her son.

"Small Richard is very happy to be seeing his King and brother this day," she smiled. "I have told him that you will see him safely to the Tower, where Edward is currently residing."

Richard grinned and looked at the man. A queasy feeling rose in the pit of the man's gut as he looked at the trusting and innocent face of the young lad. It was one thing to enrich oneself through war or guile against another adult, but quite another, he now realized, to accept reward for evil actions against a child. Small Richard slipped his hand in full trust into the paw of the Lord Protector's minion. Shame rose higher and higher. He closed his eyes a moment to regain his original sense of purpose.

"Yes, lad, we go to see your brother."

"Our King!" Richard replied solemnly. There was no response.

Elizabeth hugged him tightly.

"Mama, you are squeezing me!"

"Now, tell your brother how much I love him."

A nod.

"And remember, small Richard, how much I love you."

The man and the boy turned and walked away. Elizabeth watched them go, her heart overflowing with sadness. Her boys would find happiness in one another's company. They might think on imprisonment but she was certain that such small children would not dwell upon death. She went to the chapel to pray.

*****

Edward IV screamed in ecstasy.

"Brother! Brother!"

Small Richard ran to him and hugged him as tightly as Elizabeth had embraced him earlier.

"Ow!" laughed Edward delightedly.

"That is from Mama!"

Much later, while small Richard slept, Edward reached beneath his mattress where he had secreted the notes given to him by his brother. Lighting a small candle, he read them carefully again and again. Hours later, satisfied, he blew out the light and snuggled beneath the covers.

They would come for him - he still had friends and family and they would rescue him - the Woodvilles would not allow anything to happen to him. He was certain now. All he had to do was to look after his younger sibling and wait. His mother would come for him because she said she would. For the first time in weeks, he slept well.

Chapter Twelve

Summer 1483

Henry sat impatiently on a rocky crag overlooking the sea. On bright and cloudless days, he could actually see his homeland across the narrow channel which separated them: Brittany and France on the continental side, and beloved England gleaming like a jewel just out of reach on the other. So close!

Since the news of Edward IV's death messages had begun to arrive on a daily basis. They flooded into Brittany as from a spigot turned full bore. Initially, they were cautious and secretive as of old: they arrived by couriers dressed as priests, by ship captains and merchants ostensibly come to see some merchant of Brittany or the Duke himself.

Gradually, however, the deceits became less and less, for the simple reason that England and its crown were once again in play. Now they arrived at the front door in the keeping of official couriers of this English noble or that English priest on silver platters carried by castle servants. And there was this: Englishmen began to arrive asking to speak to

Henry or Jasper, and began declaring their allegiance to Henry Tudor. Extraordinary! Fourteen years in exile - almost half his life and now suddenly, he was no longer a bastard on the run from the English crown but a contender for its glory and power.

All of these - the messages, the messengers, the mercenaries and the noblemen all sang the same song: the king was dead; Richard was behaving not as a Lord Protector but as ruler himself; and Edward V has disappeared, his fate unknown. These were the facts to which they all attested, and it was this news upon which Henry and his uncle Jasper based their hopes and plans. Regardless of his words to the contrary, it was clear to all that Richard planned to seize the throne for himself.

How odd, thought Henry! Richard had been a loyal servant to his brother Edward IV his entire life. Not a whiff of dissatisfaction had ever floated upon the breeze, not a scintilla of revolt had ever arisen from his quarter. The man had been not just devoted to the crown, but had defended it vigorously as a brilliant general upon the battlefield. And Edward V was his own nephew - his own blood. But the accounts which now came swiftly over the channel all spoke with one voice as to the perfidy of Richard of Gloucester. And they spoke Henry's name as well, as the only man who could save the kingdom from such a monster.

Henry tore himself from his idle reverie and rose. It was late afternoon, and more messages would certainly have arrived during his absence. He gave a final glance at the channel, the chasm he must cross soon, and hurried back to the castle.

He was barely through the door when Jasper's man approached him bowing.

"Sire, sire, you are most urgently wanted by my master. You must come at once!"

Henry continued removing his gloves.

"More news from home?"

"Aye, but sire, you must hear this bit immediately."

Henry strode through a long gallery filled with tapestries and paintings, carpeted with the finest Aubusson rugs, through a narrow passageway and up a staircase which led up into his quarters. Flinging open the double doors, he found Jasper and a knot of men in furious discussion. All turned as he entered, and all bowed.

"Henry, where have you been?" Jasper waved a sheath of papers in the air. "Come, for these men have brought the most sensational news from home."

Henry poured himself a glass of ale and took up a position near the hearth before nodding. Jasper passed them to him. Before he began reading, however, Henry flipped to the last page for a signature from the author. For him, the note was only as important as its initiator. He gasped and almost dropped his drink. He looked up at Jasper and the men surrounding him.

"Buckingham!

Jasper whispered an 'aye'. Henry cast a critical eye at the men who stood with him. They wore the look of hardened warriors, men of battle. Why did Jasper seem to trust them so much? As if reading his mind, Jasper introduced his companions.

"Henry, these are Welshmen from the marches. They declare for us. They are the beginnings of our army, Henry. Now, read what Buckingham has to say."

Henry read aloud:

"My Lord Henry Tudor:

England is in dire peril. Richard of Gloucester has become a tyrant and is laying siege to our freedom. He has hidden our princes away..."

Henry paused.

"I thought he had only Edward IV?"

Jasper shook his head.

"No, he forced Elizabeth to give up small Richard as well."

Henry continued.

"No one has seen them of late. Richard has given up the black of mourning for royal purple and ermine. Daily he progresses through the streets of London with a retinue of soldiers and noblemen, waving to the crowds and dispensing alms unto them."

Henry again paused. "So he will buy the loyalty of England's masses. Oh aye, 'tis his plan."

Again from Buckingham's letter:

"I am enclosing a missive from your mother, the Lady Beaufort. She has much news as well. But I close with this, your Lordship: My troops, my lands, my people stand ready to welcome you home as our sovereign and king. All of Wales will stand with you I am certain. We stand ready, but you must hasten to act before Richard crushes the life from England. I will continue to ride at his side so as to provide you with as much information as possible."

Ever

Henry Stafford

Duke of Buckingham

Henry sat down hard. Jasper took the pages from his hand and in their stead placed two more.

"Now, read this from your mother."

"Henry my son,

Your time has arrived. It is imperative that you coordinate your battle for England's crown with Buckingham. He is of us, now, and will see you through."

She changed topics suddenly.

"I have been in touch with poor Elizabeth, our widowed queen. She still clings to sanctuary with her daughters in Westminster Abbey but agrees that a marriage between you and her daughter Elizabeth would be most advantageous for our side. It would cut vile Richard's legs straight from under him and hand him a most deserved defeat in the battle of legitimacy for the crown."

"Listen to Jasper. Stay safe, my king."

Margaret Beaufort"

Henry sat back thinking furiously of the ramifications of all he had just read. She was right - should he troth a Woodville, the late King Edward's own daughter, it would cement his claim to the throne. Richard might still be the dead king's brother, but his claim held no more merit than Henry's should that betrothal come to pass.

"And the children? Edward V and small Richard?" Henry turned to the men as he spoke.

"Henry, no one knows of them." One of the men spoke. "They have been seen on occasion in the yards of the Tower where they are held, but no one is allowed to speak to them. It is believed they are still alive, however."

"Why?" came Henry's question.

"Because even Richard would not dare kill two such innocent lambs."

Silence reigned as Henry considered the contents of the two letters. After some time, he spoke.

"And the people? Surely they are not taken in by Richard's mischief? Our people are intelligent Englishmen and they will not take usurpation of their crown lightly."

Jasper spat.

"Oh aye, you are right, but Richard has seen the same problem already."

Henry narrowed his eyes and nodded for his uncle to continue.

"Do you know the clergyman Ralph Shaa?"

"No, I do not recognize the name."

Jasper waved his hand.

"It does not matter. Last week, he preached a sermon at Paul's Cross in London."

Now it was Henry's turn to wave about.

"Get to it, uncle."

"His holy writ for the sermon was from Solomon: "Bastard slips shall not take root." And in the sermon itself, which Richard actually wrote, he declared that Edward IV had, in his youth, been betrothed ere he became married to Elizabeth, thus bastardizing Edward V and his brother small Richard."

Henry nodded. It was a clever move, he had to admit. It would make any alliance with the Woodvilles void of legitimacy in terms of lineage for the crown.

"Richard decreed that this sermon be copied and preached throughout the land so that the people might begin to view him, Richard, as England's only savior, not a base usurper."

"I see. He provides the news of his usurpation in dribs and drabbles so that they have time to accept him."

"Aye."

"But…" Henry was interrupted by a loud clattering beyond the doors to the chamber.

"I must see them now!" came a shout.

Heavy boots could be heard drawing close and every man in the room reached for his sword. Was this how it would end, Henry wondered?

But the rabble which burst upon them, tattered, tired and covered in mud followed their push into the hall by kneeling. Henry could almost hear the sigh of relief which ran round his companions. Before anyone moved, he stepped forward.

"I am Henry Tudor. What do you want? Why do you disturb us thus?"

Jasper smiled to himself - so the boy had become the king.

One of their rank stood and from within his cloak pulled a small leather pouch bound securely with leather straps. He held it forward to Henry. Henry seized the moment.

"You are tired, sir, as are your fellows."

Henry turned to the two servants who hovered against a far wall in the shadows.

"You there! Get these men some food and drink immediately. And see to their horses as well."

They scurried away.

"Tell your men they may take their ease. Food will arrive shortly."

Without waiting for anyone, Henry moved to the fire and opened the pouch, pulling from within yet another message. All waited. He finished and passed it to his uncle.

Ale arrived in two great casks and the newcomers began to relax around the tables provided. Water and cloths were brought for them to wipe their faces and boots, and shortly afterwards trays of meat, bread and candied fruit arrived. A sense of camaraderie, of union, settled upon them all.

Henry spoke to their leader and to Jasper and his men.

"So now he has Parliament on his side as well, um?"

But the leader shook his head.

"No, we do not believe he does. Not yet at least."

Henry glanced back at the missive.

"It says that a delegation of Parliamentarians marched to Richard's palace – Baynard's Castle – and offered him the crown. 'Tis the very definition of being on 'someone's side', is it not?"

Again, the leader shook his head.

"Not everyone is aboard, sire. And I have news beyond the missive: the man who led the delegation to Richard at Baynard's was none other than Buckingham."

Jasper stepped forward.

"What do you know of Buckingham?" he demanded.

The man smiled.

"I know that he is playing a dangerous game so that Henry…" here he turned and bowed slightly, "…might be crowned as our rightful king."

"But why? Why does he do this? Has he not been enriched beyond measure by Richard?" asked Henry.

"Aye, that he has, but Henry Stafford also has a conscience, and 'tis pricking his soul now."

Henry listened thoughtfully.

"Do you believe me, sire?" the man asked.

Both Henry and Jasper nodded assent as did the men behind them.

"Then, sire, I have been instructed to provide you with one more letter from Buckingham."

He clicked his fingers and a man rose from a nearby table. He handed a folded note to the leader who in turn passed it to Henry. He opened it and read aloud.

"If you are reading this, then my men have found you worthy and are confident in your leadership and discretion."

Henry looked up and again, those who late arrived bowed. He continued reading.

"That being so, I tell you that in October of this year we shall rise against the usurper Richard, and we ask that you, our rightful sovereign, join us and take your seat upon our throne as our king."

The room began to buzz.

*****

The next morning just before dawn, Henry made his way once again to the sea. Alone, he considered the wild events of the previous day and the weeks before that. So he would vie for the crown with Richard of Gloucester. And Edward V? Henry knew that should the child appear, he might have to relinquish the throne to him, but this did not disturb him in the least. His actions would be perceived as having brought down Richard the Usurper, and while the crown might slip through his fingers, surely riches and gratitude everlasting would be his compensation. Either way, he would be home among his own people, he would have a life not spent running from one refuge to another but a true home.

Still, the actions of Buckingham disturbed him deeply. What would cause a man to betray such a trust as that obviously placed in him by Richard? What had happened? And could he, Henry, trust the man? He must, and he knew it, for late in the previous evening the discussion had turned away from the logistics of Henry's conquering return to England in October to the financing of such an undertaking. Henry had no money, few if any resources beyond his connections and relatives back home. Buckingham promised him support, both in terms of men and money. Without such backing, Henry knew that the enterprise would be doomed to failure. And so he trusted because there was no other choice.

His mind ran back years, to a day he preferred not to remember. It had been cold, rainy, when the priest arrived. He was the emissary of Edward IV, and had convinced Francis, his patron, that he only wished Henry Tudor back in England in order to marry him to his daughter, thus ending all dynastic questions. Henry was not so gullible. He feigned illness, forcing the illegitimate party of English abductors into a stopover in a small village to allow for his recovery. He had escaped but only just, and the experience had seared a warning on his soul: never trust, never trust, never trust. And yet, would he now be king, he must.

As he looked out over the channel, he wished for a sign from on high. Anything would do, just an omen that this time, this day, this was right and good and God was with him. But the clouds did not part, nor did the wind shift. The waves continued to crash beneath him and the birds to circle above him. He would have to trust, and not just men, but God. Perhaps, he mused, faith, not trust, was what was required.

It was the last time he went to the sea alone. He walked the lonely forest back to the castle in full understanding of what was soon to come.

Chapter Thirteen

Thomas felt the slow rise of the road in his back before he saw it with his eyes. The day was hot and it had been a long pilgrimage back from London to Leicester. Situated northwest of the capital, Leicester sat not far from the Welsh marches, that boundary of land between the two worlds. While the area was known for its wide swaths of bogs and fens, the little town itself was built upon dry land. As he crested the knoll, Thomas saw the fleck on the distant horizon he knew to be his home. He paused happily to drink the last of the ale in his flask. What a trip it had been! He could hardly wait to share all he had learned with his friend and mentor.

Another hour brought him on to the outskirts of the village. If he squinted he could just make out old Agnes' figure in the orchard, pulling mid-season plums from the trees. She liked to preserve them while a bit of acidity remained within, saying that only the tartness of problems made us appreciate the sweetness of God's solutions. Thomas did not agree with her, thinking that God would not mind, might even approve in fact, of sweet plums but he dared not voice his thoughts on that subject to Agnes.

In the large garden adjacent to the orchard he saw an army of small children pulling weeds and hoeing under the watchful eye of a parish member. How many times had he himself been part of that brigade, helping supply the good father, now the bishop, with his winter larder. Farther on, coming in off the commons he observed a flock of twelve or so sheep being herded towards the barn for the evening. Their wool supplied coin and their bodies food, and it was well understood that should their own supply prove inadequate, the bishop could be counted upon to make sure that no child or adult in the parish went hungry. This rubbed Agnes the wrong way, who was always quick to point out that if she could manage the bishop's small estate and have such plenty, then why could they not do the same with their own? Charity was not her greatest strength.

Pausing to rub her back, she happened to glance down the road. Thomas saw her raise her hand to shield her eyes while she tried to see who was coming their way. Once certain it was him, she called out and small children came running to take her baskets of fruit to the drying shed while she disappeared indoors. The door was open for him as he finally completed his journey.

Indoors, the bishop waited in his usual chair by the fire. Agnes busied herself looking after the old man and warming water for Thomas' feet. She filled a shallow and wide bucket and placed it in front of his chair as soon as he sat. Providing him a cloth she disappeared and the bishop watched happily and silently as Thomas shed his shoes, dipped the cloth in the clean water and wiped his face repeatedly. Only then did he rest his feet comfortably in the warm liquid.

"Aaahhhhh," his sigh was one of such utter contentment that the bishop chuckled.

"'Tis good to be home, is it not?"

Thomas said nothing but winked at the old man as he wriggled his toes to loosen the dirt and grime which had accompanied him all the way from London.

After a long moment, he reached beside his chair and pulled his leather pouch - homemade and rough - onto his lap. From there he took a small, bound manuscript. The bishop's eyes lit up like a child presented with a new toy.

"Ooh, my son," he said excitedly, "You did it! You convinced the old codger to loan it to us!"

"Indeed," intoned Thomas, leaning back and closing his eyes, "...but it was not easy. He stated that if it were not once again in his possession by Yuletide, he would ride here to fetch it back himself."

Agnes reappeared with a tray of food and a comfortable silence fell as they ate. Only afterwards did Thomas begin to discuss what he had seen and heard in London.

"The news across the kingdom and from London, 'tis bad, bishop, bad indeed."

"The king? Edward V?"

Thomas shook his head and Agnes clucked from her chair near the fire.

"No one has seen him or his brother for some time."

"His brother! I thought Queen Elizabeth had got him clean away from Richard and into sanctuary in the Abbey!"

"Aye," came Thomas' reply, "But pressure was put upon the good queen to release him from the holy place. It is said on the street that Richard assured her that small Richard would be sent to comfort the new king, and that she could not refuse knowing how lonely and confused Edward must be."

The bishop shook his head.

"That news is sad, but there is worse. After parading himself through London and its environs for days on end, tossing coins at the crowd like a mad fool, he has had the audacity to have himself crowned.

Agnes and the bishop gasped.

"'Tis true," said Thomas. "I would not have believed it but on the very day I was leaving on my return journey to Leicester, I got caught up in the crowd which gathered to watch it."

He poured himself more ale and continued.

"'Twas the sixth of July, it was. Richard, that evil usurper, marched to the Abbey barefoot with his wife, whom he now styles Queen Anne. Oh, the pageantry was so gaudy as to make one queasy. Queen Anne even had her own retinue - her own household! Richard's troops - or the crown's troops - were posted along the way, and those who did mumble dissent were whisked away. God help those poor bastards."

Agnes gasped.

"And the boys?" asked Agnes. "What will happen to them now?"

The bishop shook his head before answering.

"They are in peril, you may rest assured. But as great and sorrowful as that is, 'tis the kingdom that is my greatest concern, for if the crown has passed to one who was not destined to wear it and rule, then England may see yet more civil war."

All three shuddered.

"What of Edward, Richard's own son?" asked Agnes.

Thomas shrugged.

"No one sees much of him. 'He is not close to his father'…'Tis all that is said."

"Dear Lord in heaven," said Agnes, "We cannot have more war, for the last one - twixt the Lancasters and the Yorks - nearly proved the ruin of England. Aye, we were ripe for the plucking by some continental power. 'Tis only the grace of God which saved us all."

The bishop smiled reassuringly at her.

"French is not our official tongue yet, Agnes, nor will it ever be." He paused. "Perhaps it would have been better if we *had* seen an invasion from distant shores. At least that would have served to unite *our* two warring houses against a common and foreign enemy."

Thomas stood and arched his back.

"I am worn and need sleep. I choose not to dwell on the absolute evil which is abroad. I choose instead to focus on my manuscripts and my languages. Did you know, bishop, that I believe I have found a hitherto unreported scholia in Exodus? Very exciting!"

"Indeed!" came the old man's excited reply. "I can hardly wait!"

Agnes looked at the two of them and shook her head.

"'Tis nothing but manuscripts and goodwill and cheer and love in this house."

Both men laughed.

"Aye, so what are you so sour about?"

"My knowledge of the world is far greater than the two of yours combined. You may read and write and Lord knows what with your books and pens and ink, but I know better. Should hard times fall they fall on the good and the evil alike. No one escapes."

She continued muttering dire warnings beneath her breath. Thomas smiled.

"Ah, 'tis good to be home."

The bishop nodded in agreement and with the aid of his cane, hobbled slowly off to bed.

Chapter Fourteen

Late July 1483

Richard paced anxiously in the King's Hall of Westminster Palace. He had counted out the number of square marble floor slabs from wall to wall, and to calm his mind he recounted them each time as he went to and fro. And each time he reached the end of the row, he turned and adjusted his caplet before beginning again. It was a new device - a short cloak of sorts - which his valet had designed. It would not do for his subjects to view their new king as physically impaired, and with the help of the voluminous caplet, he was better able to hide his shoulder.

'Their new king'! He rolled the phrase round and round in his head, enjoying the sound of it. What a great and wonderful thing he had accomplished for himself, and of course, for the kingdom. He still could almost not believe it and growing tired of pacing while waiting, he sat by the hearth to relive the recent glory days of his rise to absolute power.

His most favorite memory was the coronation. Such splendor! It had not been as difficult to arrange as he had imagined. The vast state machinations required to feed, clothe, house and equip those who participated in his many parades had already been put in motion by the time of his acceptance of the crown. It had been a simple matter of re-sizing the actual crown for him rather than for Edward's bastard son.

He remembered fondly the delegation from Parliament as they beseeched him at Baynard's Castle to accept the crown for the glory and safety of the realm. Really, so eloquent had been their request, so effusive were they in their pleadings, well, he could hardly have said no. And so much wealth! He thought of how satisfied he had been as the Duke of Gloucester, brother to good King Edward, and almost laughed aloud at his own naiveté. How had that been possible, he now wondered? Kingship endowed him with ten, twenty times the wealth he had possessed before. Ah, it had been adequate he believed and then some - had he not been the second wealthiest man in the kingdom at that point? But now, possessing as he did so much more, he could see how foolish he had been.

There was more glory in kingship than just property, however. Glory and light oozed out of the words addressed to him by all: "your highness, my sovereign" and on and on; the clothing which adorned him and the jewels for each outfit screamed power to all; but most of all, glory sat quietly by his side now at all times, giving him an aura of pure, unadulterated power and authority. God's liver, it was fine indeed.

As always, though, when he allowed his thoughts to drift, unwelcome images of his brother's sons, Edward and small Richard appeared. Indeed, it was because of them that he paced and gnawed his fingernails this very morning. But as a heavy knock came at the door on the far end of the hall, Richard banished thoughts of them. They had been found to be bastards and the news had been bruited abroad to the kingdom at large. It was enough that he had saved their lives. What to do with them long-term, well, that would have to wait for the simple reason he did not know what to do with them. His choices were stark. Let them live? Send them abroad to a far-away land…where their very existence was bound to call into question his own kingship? But the alternative, well…

The Duke of Buckingham strode purposefully towards him and Richard was pleased to see him stop at some distance from his royal person and bow deeply. Yes, fine indeed it was to be king.

"News?" He asked quickly.

"It is put down."

A sigh of relief escaped Richard's lips. He called for drinks and when they arrived dismissed all but Buckingham.

"Well, it was bound to be a failure, was it not?"

Buckingham appeared to think for a moment, and Richard noticed for the first time that his friend seemed to have trouble making eye contact.

"Is there something you wish to say?" he asked coldly.

Buckingham finally spoke.

"The rescue attempt this morning of the two boys was well-planned, Majesty. The men who breeched the Tower defenses were well-informed and equally well-armed. It was only serendipity that they were not successful."

Richard sat up, listening more intently.

"Had Edward and small Richard been in their rooms, they would have been rescued…"

"Stop using that word!" Richard shouted.

Buckingham nodded.

"…only because they were playing in the small yard behind the main tower when the attack occurred was it not successful and they were not…taken."

"Meaning..." prompted Richard.

"The children usually have tutorials at that time of day, but their tutor had declared a holiday for them because of lessons well-learned in previous days. Only this caused the operation to fail."

Richard's blood begin to run cold.

"So it was not a frivolous, ill-planned abduction scheme after all. It came from those with power and knowledge."

"Aye," Buckingham agreed, "But we shall never know who."

"And why not?"

"The guards on duty were killed in the attack, and the men who launched it escaped. By the time a secondary force responded to the bell alarm, they were gone."

Richard stroked his chin furiously. His shoulder began to ache with a vengeance.

"And the boys? Where are they now?"

"Still in the Tower, Majesty."

"Well, move them deeper into the place - use the old quarters that were reserved for my late brother. It would be difficult indeed to breech *these*."

Buckingham nodded and changed the subject.

"'Tis not the children that you should worry about, Majesty. 'Tis the mood of your people."

"What mood?" Richard spoke dryly. "I throw money at them daily. I make sure they are entertained with circuses and food and drink. They will not cause trouble."

Buckingham's silence grated on Richard.

"Speak your mind, man." He commanded.

"Sire, only the guards which lined the streets at your coronation stopped them from hurling insults at you and your gracious Queen Anne. They take your coin, your entertainment, and will continue to do so, aye, but that will not stop them from murmuring what they perceive as the truth."

Richard raised an eyebrow expectantly.

"Usurpation." The word fell like stone upon stone.

Richard threw his glass at the fire.

"Damn them! A *child* – a *mere boy* could never handle the crown or the responsibilities that come with it. *Never, do you hear me?"*

Buckingham held his peace as Richard raged on.

"How ungrateful these people are. I have spared them a *child king* who would open us up to vast schemes and manipulations and wars and all in the name of peace. *Fools! I alone* have saved them all that by assuming what was rightfully mine - *mine,* do you hear? *Mine!*"

Small globs of spittle appeared at the corners of his mouth.

"And as for the commoners, I will throw no more money at them. And nobles who stand with me must beg for crown lands now. I will NOT be used and I will NOT be thwarted and denied what is rightfully mine. How many years, how many battles, did I fight for this kingdom? It is MINE, I tell you."

Buckingham rose.

"You will do as I say and move the bastard children! And you will preach unto the ranks of lackeys who do my bidding and eat at my table that should they should tread carefully, lest I learn that they personally do not care for my rule."

Buckingham bowed deeply on one knee.

"I stand with you, my sovereign. You know that."

His words seemed to settle Richard somewhat.

"Yes, yes, I know. 'Tis the others we have to be watchful of." He sat tiredly, his shoulder clearly twitching beneath the caplet.

"That is all. Leave me."

Buckingham did as commanded, but as he pulled the heavy oaken doors behind him, he could not help but smile inwardly.

"Richard, you do not understand your people." He spoke the words softly. "No, you do not. Oh, aye, I too will take the gifts you shower upon me for helping you usurp what is not yours, but do not expect loyalty, for that cannot be bought."

He paused on the great stairs.

"And as for the children, no Majesty, I will not help you there. You must ride alone with only evil as your co-conspirator should you choose to harm innocents. Again a pause. "Come Henry - your time is well-nigh. You will protect the innocents and give us a moral and just ruler."

*****

"What are you doing?"

Agnes put her hand on a nearby table and hoisted herself up from kneeling.

"Why?" she looked at him almost defiantly.

"Well, 'tis not everyday I see you on the floor." For the first time, he noticed the small hole that Agnes had hollowed out of the packed dirt. Without a word, he looked askance at her. She wiped her hands, poured them both a drink and sat at the small table.

"'Tis for winter stores."

"We have a root cellar, Agnes. Are you going dotty?" Thomas laughed at his little joke.

"You laugh now, old man, but you will not should hard times come."

"I do not understand."

"Anything in our root cellar will be taken away or burned when they burn the roof over our heads."

"God's knees, Agnes! What is wrong with you?"

She pointed to the hole in the floor.

"I shall lay a larder away that only we will know of. That way, should the day come when this house is in need, I - and I alone (she emphasized the alone as though shaming him while pointing her finger at his face) - will have had the forethought to plan for hard times."

She nodded and sliced a piece of ham for herself. Munching contentedly, she continued.

"Aye, you will thank me then I imagine. Save your laughter, Thomas. Clearly you only have eyes for your manuscripts and scraps of paper, but I see clearly what is happening."

"And what is that, Agnes." Thomas sat back and waited for her usual doomsday tone and story. She did not disappoint.

"Have you not looked around, man? At the market? People are selling only what they have to in order to survive. The rest of the crops are being hoarded in holes just like that one!" she nodded to her handiwork.

"And the hoarding does not stop there. Anything that might fetch a price should the day come and coin is needed, well, you will not see such items in the market place anytime soon. Aye, there is a darkness coming, Thomas. You wait and see."

Thomas shrugged and smiled before leaving her to her digging.

She was right and he knew it. He was not observant, and that was what worried him. If even he in his constant state of fog had noticed that supplies in the market were not what they should be, then Agnes was right. And he had seen it for weeks now. He had noticed, too, the quiet whispers among the merchants, the worried looks on the faces of those with large families and small farms –

the pinched look on the concerned faces of parents as they looked at their children.

Indeed, he thought sadly, a pall was settling over the land. And really, what else should be expected. A usurpation of their crown had occurred, but not just any usurpation. The rightful king was a child, and his heir would be his younger brother. Both of them had disappeared now, and no one dared speak their names.

England had deserted her rightful monarch, and in return for that was now cursed with a deceitful and evil ruler.

He sighed, wondering what would come.

*****

As they sat by the fire, Edward and small Richard tossed dice and rolled marbles at play. They were in new quarters, the ones once used by their father himself whenever he had chosen to stay at the Tower. The rooms were large and well-lit; the floors were covered in ancient rugs and the walls hung with priceless tapestries.

Edward believed their happier circumstances were due directly to his mother's intervention. After all, she was the widow of a king and the mother of another - him! Yes, he was certain she was in the process of setting things right. She had explained in one of the notes sent via small Richard that they were secreted away in the Tower because there was trouble in the land, that many, many usurpers of his crown had risen and now vied with one another in pointless battle. He, Edward V, the rightful king, was being kept safe so that when the carnage ended, he could be brought forth. How happy his subjects would be!

And so for now, he and small Richard played their games and learned their lessons.

It would not be long now, he was certain.

"Brother," an exasperated and childish voice broke his thoughtful reverie, "Edward! It is your turn - do you not see?"

Edward smiled at his brother.

"Indeed! Well, I shall take it now, for the sooner I take it, the sooner I beat you!"

Small Richard smiled happily.

Chapter Fifteen

September 1483

It happened at the morning mass. A small thing, really, nothing remarkable. Richard was only just hearing the priest's admonitions concerning the third beatitude when he realized that the man was focusing on the latter part:

"Blessed are the meek..."

Fine, fine, thought Richard and stretched his legs to relieve his boredom.

"...For they shall inherit the earth."

Richard's ears pricked up. Had the man deliberately stressed the latter part...*they shall inherit the earth*? He was almost certain that he had. He began to listen intently. On and on droned the good father, discussing the importance of women's attitudes towards their husbands and fathers and brothers; the necessity of meekness before one's social betters; even subservience to one's liege as a tenant farmer. But there was no mention of obedience to king and crown.

Richard coughed loudly and rose as though to adjust his clothing, all the while drilling a hole into the priest's soul with a cold stare that surely contained an unspoken threat.

The clergyman looked down at his notes in terror and then raised a trembling voice.

"And of course, no allegiance is more important than allegiance to God and King."

Richard gave an almost imperceptible nod and sat back down. The priest rambled on for some time, reiterating the words Richard had silently commanded him to speak. After some time, he once again lost interest and returned to his own thoughts, which primarily concerned the dinner he would enjoy immediately following the service.

He thought nothing more of the priest's oversight - after all, he was likely saving that bit for the last, to finish on a high note that would stay with his congregation.

But last week, some low clod of a nobleman - no doubt promoted during Richard's haste to give largesse to those whom he needed - had seen fit to interrupt him while he was speaking.

"I would like the alms I provide today to be of smaller weight for I think..."

"Almsman, see to it!" called forth the minor nobleman from the back of the hall. Richard looked at him but the man seemed not to notice. And then…

"Yes, majesty? You were saying?"

Richard could not believe the ignorance and utter lack of humble servitude thus displayed. Buckingham saw and sensed what was happening and immediately gave a deep and lasting bow. Taking his lead, everyone else in the room did likewise. Only after a long minute did Buckingham rise, turn to the idiot and whisper softly to those who stood next to him. Without a word, they stalked to the miscreant, grabbed him by the arms and escorted him from the hall. Richard was placated. He made a mental note to have Buckingham emphasize to his guard the proper forms of protocol towards his royal person. Such incidents so early in his reign were bound to occur. The hearing had continued without further incident.

But the third small thing - the third not remarkable thing in as many weeks - had kicked him in the midsection like an angry mule. He had been riding at Greenwich, hunting in the wood which he could now claim as his own. He had no need to ask permission to bring down the largest stag there or anywhere else.

The early morning hunt had proved dissatisfying, and he finished with no game save a small pheasant. After venting his displeasure with his beaters and yeomen, he had taken the road to

London immediately. He had no wish to return his mount to the stable and be shown empty-handed to all his servants, let alone the noble court that had progressed with him thence. No, to London.

A hard ride brought him to Baynard's Castle and he laughed inwardly as the servants there scrambled and panicked at his unexpected appearance. In his usual way of things, a retinue of courtiers and guards, of administrators and clerks, rode ahead to announce one of his coming visits to any venue, if only for a day or an afternoon. This gave the hosting nobleman or his own servants time to prepare, to beat the rugs or throw down fresh rushes, to bathe and put on their finest livery. It gave the kitchens time to prepare a meal fit for a king and up to several hundred members of his court. In short, the accustomed advance notice may have served as a courtesy to the lesser men of his estates, but its true purpose was to ensure the king's own comfort.

This day, seeing the antics and the chaos created by his unheralded arrival, he eschewed the usual grand entrance as well. He clucked and shook his head as a man raced forward in an attempt to get in front of him and throw open the huge entry doors to the central hallway. Instead Richard, silently chuckling to himself, inched open one heavy door and slid silently in. The grand hall was dark and poorly lit, and after giving his eyes time to adjust, he looked around.

The room ran the entire width of the castle, essentially cutting its major wings into two distinct halves. It was a full sixty feet from the door to the marbled stairwell which gave onto the second floor. So far away, in fact, was the stairwell that the two men upon it, hunched and in serious conversation, had neglected to notice his entry into Baynard's or his stealthy approach towards them now.

Richard had recognized Henry Stafford even from a distance for the simple reason that he was wearing his usual burnt umber cloak, dark hosiery and cobalt blue pantaloons. It was his favorite suit, apparently, for he wore it often. But that was not that which continued to draw Richard's attention.

Some transaction was taking place. The man speaking with Buckingham repeatedly cast furtive glances all about. The fact that Richard did not recognize him, and that he was dressed in a simple priest's frock, was odd. And Buckingham himself was acting strangely. He had in his hand some small package - a scrolled paper? A beige-colored bag? - Richard could not tell. The floor creaked suddenly beneath his weight, both men turned, and it was at that moment that Richard's subconscious went to work.

Faster than lightning, the man took the package from Buckingham and tucked it deep within his priestly robes. Both men bowed deeply and then advanced to Richard now at the foot of the stairway.

"Now be gone!" Buckingham spoke loudly to the man at his side. "Take the alms our good king provides and distribute them today in his name."

Without waiting for Buckingham to finish, the man gave a frightened bow to Richard and first skipped, then lightly ran down the hall and out the front doors. He was gone in the blink of an eye.

Richard looked at Buckingham thoughtfully while servants now appeared and peeled his cloak and hat from his body. He was still dressed for the hunt and Buckingham raised an eyebrow. Richard noted the other man's response to his present dress and now laughed himself at his own attire.

"I shall clean, and then we shall dine," he said. "And oh, by the way, who was that man? That priest."

Buckingham waved his hand airily. "Some common priest – I did not even catch his name. He asked for alms for some good cause and I supplied him with coin. 'Tis typical these days, your majesty, for you are known for the care and love you feel for your subjects."

Buckingham coughed and rubbed this throat before continuing.

"Sire, I beg you to allow me to leave your presence and go to my country home. I have a chill and my throat aches. I would not wish to be the man who might pass along such a malady as these things portend to our sovereign lord."

Richard nodded.

"No, indeed. Leave, then, and when you are well, we will meet again."

Buckingham bowed and walked in stately measure to the great doors. Some servant opened them for him and Richard heard him calling for his mount as they closed behind him.

Once upstairs, his valet appeared and scullery children began filling the great bathing tub with hot water. In accord with Richard's physician's wishes, lavender, rose hips and chips of the dried bark of a willow tree were added to the water. Before stepping in, the valet used one bucket of scalding water to rub and wash the dirt from his frame. Only then did Richard step into the tub for a long soothing soak.

"I wish you to find something out for me." He spoke to his valet as the man assisted him in getting comfortable.

"Majesty?"

"I wish to know who the priest on the stairs was just now with Buckingham."

"The valet bowed, spoke a curt reminder to the children to continue heating water, and walked quickly from the room. A servant appeared a few moments later with a cup of wine for Richard. He left the decanter and the tray on a small table adjacent to the tub and bowed his way from the room. Richard was alone.

He was not certain why he asked for the priest's name. Some odd jerk of movement, perhaps, on the stairwell? Had he pocketed the mysterious package too quickly perhaps? Did the man avoid looking him in the eye directly? And he had left in a hurry, without even thanking Richard for the alms. Altogether, it was odd, coming on the heels of a day Richard felt was off kilter somehow already. He had shot no stag, ridden hard for Baynard's for no particular reason, and Buckingham had claimed illness, something he had never done before in Richard's presence. And so he had asked.

Much later, the valet returned with the brigade of children with more buckets. While some scooped the now cooling liquid from the tub, others poured in the freshly heated water. Richard closed his eyes and started on his second drink. When the children were gone, the valet spoke.

"Majesty, I have ascertained the information you requested about the priest."

"Oh?" He sat up straighter in the bath. "Indeed, well, who was he then?"

"He is a priest, Sire, attached to the service of a noblewoman."

Richard sensed hesitancy.

"And the noblewoman's name?"

The valet bowed deeply, as though the act would protect him from the words he now spoke.

"Margaret Beaufort, Majesty, the mother of the exiled Henry."

Richard realized unreservedly that something was afoot. It was too much to believe that such events were all separate, unlinked by some common malevolent thread. It wasn't that they were directly connected, but they represented…what…a lessening of respect, a willingness to look beyond Richard as king, perhaps, to him who would be so next? They pointed to a shadow approaching his throne, tentatively and obliquely. Indeed, if he had not witnessed these three disturbing events in such short order, he would not have realized it. But what was 'it'?

Then, like a sudden epiphany, Richard suddenly saw the whole picture clearly. He finally understood what had been nagging at his mind for some weeks now. An uncontrollable shout of rage escaped his lips and the valet turned to flee, but just as quickly Richard shouted again, this time for the man to stay. Trembling and bowing, the valet did so.

"You will tell no one, of this information. Do you understand?"

The frightened man nodded fervently.

"And whoever you told of this, isolate them now in my hearing chamber. Tell them I wish to speak to them."

Again, the man's head bobbed in frantic up and down motion.

He ran from the room and Richard sank into the hot bath once again.

So Henry Stafford, the mighty Duke of Buckingham, would plot against him. Richard spat in disgust: was there no man, no human who walked the face of the earth, who was not perfidious? Who was not a Janus to his own monarch? What did Buckingham think to gain from rebellion? For it could only mean rebellion, if he were sending secret messages to Henry Tudor's own mother. He could fathom what the man thought he might gain, but it must be vastly superior to what he had been given by Richard. He spat again, drained his cup and slid down into the still hot water, feeling its soothing touch lap over his body.

A wicked smile lit his thin features as he brushed the damp hair off his forehead. Henry Stafford might best him at scheming; he might even best Richard at plotting. But at rebellion? Oh no. That would never happen. Richard had spent his life securing the kingdom against this insurrection or that uprising. He may have been duped by his closest advisor, but on a battlefield, Richard never lost. He understood command in the face of terror, attack in the face of seemingly impossible odds, the need for caution and cunning against a wily adversary. No. There was no one who could match him in force of arms, on a field of battle, and he knew it well enough.

And it was there, on a battlefield somewhere, that the grand Duke of Buckingham would fall, and with him his rebellion. Usurp his crown? Richard rose, laughed, and threw his glass into the fire. He felt the fury of the coming battle in his bones - he always enjoyed the calm before the storm.

The question now was a simple one. How far had the plot advanced? Did Henry Tudor know of it? He pulled on his chemise without the help of a valet and sat before the fire until dawn.

Chapter Sixteen

Early October, 1483

On the surface, nothing about Richard or his routine had changed. He split his time between Baynard's Castle and Westminster Palace when in London, and at Greenwich when he wished to progress. Even when he learned that Buckingham had indeed retired not just to the country but to Brecon Castle, his Welsh estate near the boundary marches, he said nothing untoward. And the fact that Henry Tudor could be expected to draw heavily for support from Wales - after all, he was a bastard Welshman - even that seemed not to disturb the king. Beneath the surface, however, there was roiling activity.

He reached out to the men who had fought side by side with him most recently in Scotland. These were not men he had to purchase - they had proven their loyalty to him over time and in battle. They were brothers in arms. Responding to the cryptic and secret notes sent out to them by Richard, they came one by one to London. There was James Harrington, a good and loyal man, and John Howard and William Parr. John de la Pole, his own nephew, answered the call immediately. And these soldiers came not alone, but with troop commitments and arms as well.

Richard had given considerable thought to the clergy, for it was through them that much of his control of the populace of his realm flowed. They would follow the church, and so the church must follow Richard. With bribes, with pre-written sermons which foretold fire and chaos should the king not be secure upon the throne, and suggestions for other, similar sermons, with solicitous care and veiled threats he cajoled them to do his bidding should they ever have to choose sides. They received promises and more. His missives also painted in stark tones the dire futures awaiting them should they not stand with him.

Richard had been careful to give Buckingham adequate time to recover, and, to assume that he was away clean with his treasonous plans. Then, as though inquiring of an old friend's health, he wrote him a charming epistle, and invited him to Westminster for discussions of the realm and how best to rule it. Four days later, a response arrived: the Duke was always at the king's service, but the chill and the sore throat had become a chest-deep cough, one to which he dared not expose the king and his court.

He allowed three days to pass upon receipt of the information which he knew to be false. On the fourth, he wrote again, demanding that Henry

Stafford, Duke of Buckingham, present himself forthwith, cough or no cough. The message went unanswered, for Buckingham had been involved in far too many similar maneuverings to think that Richard had nothing but good in his heart towards him at this point. It seemed to both sides that the battle had been joined.

And Henry Tudor? Of him, nothing was known. Richard had set a watch upon Margaret Beaufort but the woman was too clever by half. Buckingham had no doubt warned her and she was careful to maintain her image of the epitome of grace and godly devotion to church and crown.

Uneasy and unconvinced, Richard sent several 'priests' to Brittany and dispatched an official party to Frances, the duke who ruled the tiny kingdom. The intelligence reports which came to him daily now suggested that the troops and men of the uprising were scattered across the southern portion of England, whether to trick him into dividing his own armies into smaller, more easily defeated bites, or whether because the men who controlled them chose that strategy for other reasons he could not fathom. He refused to rise to the bait regardless, instead choosing to move the bulk of his men to Salisbury for a confrontation with Buckingham: he relished the idea. Other troops were sent to Surrey, to the village of Guildford, sure to be a rebel stronghold. Should the need arise to hold the south against the traitors, a sizeable contingent was sent on to Leicester.

As he rode out from London on October 9th, word reached him from one of the messengers he had sent abroad: Henry Tudor had assembled a small force and a flotilla to ferry them to England. It was rumored that the Duke of Brittany was his financier.

England, it seemed, would be plunged into yet another civil war after all.

*****

October 10, 1483

Fifteen ships, five thousand men, 10,000 golden ducats! Henry stood on the Brittany coast surveying his small army in the bay before him. All of it was due to Francis, Duke of Brittany, who was betting on this young exile to capture the English crown. On the other side of the channel, the Duke of Buckingham had raised a mighty army to help him seize the throne. Upon receiving word that Henry intended to sail this day, he had set his own men and plans in motion.

But Richard, long privy to the schemes and dreams which surrounded him, was also prepared. He would first take down Buckingham and crush his co-conspirators beneath his heel. And then, as for Henry Tudor, the man had been abroad too long, let him come home and meet his overdue fate.

Strangely, nearly identical sentiments ran through Henry Tudor's mind that day. As he looked behind him over the stern of the bark shoving off from the coast of Brittany, he saw his state of exile fast disappearing. And as he turned and looked forward from the prow, he saw his future forming in the melting mist of England's chalky coast.

*****

November 1, 1483

But it all came to naught. A comic failure of a rebellion and an equally ludicrous attempt at invasion from the continent.

Richard should have been content. After all, his crown was now secure. But Henry Tudor had slipped through his grasp, and having shown how vulnerable England was, he would surely return. This fact, more than any other, began to worm its way slowly into the depths of his soul.

Henry Stafford, the Duke of Buckingham, was no more. At the final moment he had fled, disguised as a common man. His aim: to reach the sea and from thence to Brittany to support Henry Tudor. But his own gave him up, a testament to his shoddy treatment of his tenants and servants, and he was beheaded at the executioner's block.

And Henry Tudor. What began as a voyage of triumphant return and the seizing of a crown which was rightfully his had all come crashing down most unceremoniously. As his small fleet passed the halfway mark on the rolling channel, a storm approached, and like Odysseus at the whim of the winds released from Aeolus' pouch, the ships were scattered and lost. Only Henry's managed to make the appointed time and place of rendezvous on the English coast. And yes, there on the coast to greet him were Buckingham's men, cheering and waving exuberantly.

But Henry hesitated. Jasper by his side also paused. They spoke quietly so that the others might not hear.

"Something is wrong, I feel it," Jasper spoke in undertones. "Why are they shouting and beckoning to us thus? Should they not be quiet and wary, lest Richard discover us before we are ready?"

Henry shook his head in agreement.

"Let us send a dory nearby to shore. They will be able to ascertain better if they can see the men face to face."

Jasper agreed and ten men were dispatched in a small landing boat. The oarsmen pulled mightily, and within a few minutes they were within hailing distance yet still out of reach of treachery. Henry and Jasper watched anxiously.

Suddenly, without warning, the dory turned and began a furious retreat towards the main ship. Jasper turned to the men behind him.

"Get the anchor up! Set the sails now! Move...*quickly*!"

The shouting on shore turned to angry bellowing as arrows began to splash into the water just shy of smaller vessel. No sooner had it reached the ship than they were off, leaving the empty dory floating upon an equally empty sea.

"What happened? What did you learn?" Henry and Jasper asked the breathless men upon their return.

"They are Richard's men, come to take us captive."

"How do you know?"

The lead man pointed back towards the shore.

"Look yonder, over that low rise."

All within hearing squinted to see what miracle had saved them. And there, flickering in the breeze, was a small pennant. A smile went round the group. It bore Richard's insignia. But for an overeager army, they would have been lost.

*****

Three soldiers, dressed in Richard's colors and riding mighty destriers, were the last of Richard's men to leave Leicester. They had seen no battle, received no promotions or wealth for their loyal service, and were thoroughly angry as a result.

"So we are sent to Leicester - *Leicester* - while the men who rode south surely saw glorious action," spoke one.

"Aye," came the reply in unison from his two comrades.

"And they will receive promotions, pensions, annuities, estates..."

Another man took up the rant.

"Women, wealth, perhaps even royal status. Their children..."

"*Their* children," came the caustic reply from the third, "...will order *our* children into battle. *Our* children will cook for them, clean for them, and oh aye, *our* women will be subject to *their* whims."

The sky was darkening in the west and they rode wordlessly on for some while.

"So what is our plan?"

Another brief silence ensued.

"I plan to ride all night and make London tomorrow. I intend to find out what happened down south, and to see if there is still a possibility of some reward."

"And I," chimed in a second, "...will keep you company."

They turned to the last companion.

"What say ye?"

But he shook his head.

"No, I shall pull up here." He pointed to a small well-tended manor just coming into view. "I shall stop there for the night, and see you anon."

He let out a nasty chortle.

"Perhaps they have a daughter."

The others laughed and clicked their mounts to ride on. Their companion slowed and entered the narrow and rutted way leading to the manor house.

A middle-aged man responded to his persistent knocking.

"May I be of service?" He inquired politely of the soldier.

"Oh, aye, you may indeed." The soldier brushed him aside and entered a cozy sitting room filled with books and manuscripts. A wizened and white haired man sat by the fire while farther away sat a portly woman. She stared hard at the stranger without speaking. The soldier picked up the old man's cup of ale and drained it in one gulp. Seeing the decanter nearby, he poured himself another and sat in the chair opposite.

"I beg your pardon?" the middle-aged man spoke up. "You dare enter a private home and act thus?"

The soldier burped and stretched out his legs.

"I dare that and more. Tell your woman to come over here and take my boots. And I need food."

The woman did not move.

"Did you not hear me, wench?"

The woman stood.

"Oh, aye, sir, I heard you, but…"

At that moment the old man, silent until then, rose.

"Sir, you must forgive us if we seem surprised. We were not expecting a guest this evening. Pray tell us your business so that we might aid you."

The soldier poured yet another drink.

"I have no need of your aid. My king, King Richard, has just defeated those who would usurp his crown."

"The crown *he* usurped?" asked the woman innocently.

The soldier rose immediately and pulled his sword. The alcohol, the circumstances, the woman, yes, he was feeling better – the night just became interesting.

"How dare you?" he shouted at her. "Do you dare question the legitimacy of our sovereign monarch?"

She said nothing more. The soldier drank directly from the pitcher and threw it into the fire.

"I believe, old bird, that I must teach you a lesson this night." He laughed and smiled at her lasciviously. "You are not much to look upon, but you will have to do, seeing as how you are the only woman here."

He lunged in her direction but the old man was quicker.

"Stand down, man, for you are too angry and drunk to know what you propose. Let us give you food to match your ale, aye, and a warm bed in which to sleep. You will see things differently in the morn."

The soldier looked at him intently.

"Move aside!"

The threat was palpable, but the elderly man stood firm. Something rattled behind the soldier and he turned. From nowhere it seemed the middle-aged man had produced a long-sword of the sort the soldier knew had been used centuries earlier. He laughed and turned back to the woman and the man in front of her.

"Your friend back there," he moved his head to indicate the other man, "…he seems to think he can defeat me with that ancient sword. I doubt he could cut butter with the thing."

"Find out." Came the quiet words from behind. But the soldier continued to stare at the woman. Finally, raising his sword, he pointed it at the old man.

"Step aside, or I will help you do so."

"No."

"You bastard!"

It was all over in but a second. The woman shrilled the words and stepped forward as the soldier's sword whistled through the air, intent on giving a nick to the old man's arm. But the alcohol had now hit with full force on the soldier's empty stomach and he shifted ever so slightly on his feet, yielding a more deadly arc to the blade and it entered the old man's abdomen instead. The soldier seemed stunned by what had just happened but as he sought to turn a wild yell from behind caused him to lurch forward, driving the sword deeper into the wound. Without warning, the ancient blade of the other man sliced through his own chest. Old man and intruder fell together into a bloody heap on the cold stone floor.

"Dear God in heaven, dear God in heaven!" The woman knelt at the old man's side. But he could not respond. She gently closed his eyes amid the flood of tears from her own.

"Get up." She ignored the middle-aged man's cry.

"Get up, I say, for others will be here, and if we are found to have murdered a king's man we will be hung - if we are lucky."

They stood staring at one another for a long moment in their mutual grief and shock. Finally a creak from the front door still ajar made them jump and set them into furious and panicked motion. In a few breaths they were out of the door.

"But burial! We must see to it!"

"Nay, we must see to ourselves."

So sudden was the catastrophe that neither had time to think. They grabbed their cloaks in unison, the man clutched his sword and they ran for the door. Outside, the soldier's horse neighed at the sudden action. The man calmed him and swung himself up into the saddle. Reaching down, he helped the woman mount behind him.

As he turned towards the main road she hissed in his ear.

"No, no. There may be more - we do not know what he was doing in this place or how many were with him. If we are caught by his fellows on a king's horse, by God they will have us."

The man turned the animal again and it began to trot towards the back of the manor.

"Where are you going?"

"The cow trail up over the ridge. I will leave you near Leicester. Father Burress will take care of you."

"And you?"

They reached the ancient trail which ran from the market in Leicester to the manor and beyond. As he kicked the beast into a gallop, he laughed bitterly into the wind.

"I have nowhere to go! I have just murdered a man. I am lost."

They rode in silence until finally a rutted crossroads appeared in the moonlight. He pulled the animal up short and helped the woman off.

"See to yourself," he said, despair leaking around the edges of his words.

"They will hide me, fear not. But you and the horse must be gone."

He shook his head in agreement. The moonlight caught them both in silhouette, two desperate figures now on the run. He reached down and took her hand. She clasped his in both of hers.

"Strange, is it not? It all came to an end in less than the wink of an eye. Take care, Agnes."

"You as well, Thomas. And should you need me, ask at the church, for they will always know my whereabouts."

They parted. She began running towards the town as he galloped over the ridge and out of sight.

"*...murdered a man...*". The phrase kept ringing in his ears. Aye, he was lost, as was his soul as well. Tears streaked his face.

There was nothing left for him on this earth now.

Chapter Seventeen

December, Christmas Day, 1483

Rennes Cathedral

He stood to the side in the great sanctuary of the famous cathedral, barely noticing the magnificent beauty of the place. When he had traveled to the small French town of Rennes that very morning, Henry had seen it rising in the distance, heard it calling to the faithful with the somber song of heaven sung by its bells and its vivid images etched and set forth in huge stained-glass windows. Like many such fabled churches, the building had been a community work of the middle ages, its design and construction stretching over decades; before that, even, the place had been deemed holy, its history of sacred rituals and godly purpose stretching back into Roman times.

Henry felt rather than saw his men gathering in the back of the sanctuary, near the grand doors. He wanted no company at this moment, not even Jasper's, and they waited patiently for his signal.

He did not pace, but stood in deep repose, composing in his heart a narrative of the recent past.

The October invasion had been a disaster. Henry had known shame and embarrassment over the years; his penniless exile had taught him to accept, even ask for, handouts from those around him. But he had always managed to compartmentalize those events, to rationalize them as necessities of the moment – ways to move forward to the next moment, the next year, the next time when life would be better. But the failure of October was seismically different. It had involved not individual princes or dukes but nation states; it had played out not in this province or that but on an international stage; it was discussed in courts by kings and queens far and wide; it was public in ways he had not before imagined possible.

He had always been a known figure, but this, this was different. This was scrutiny the likes of which he had never known. Men and women alike now seemed to look at him differently; they assessed him, calculated him, eyed him appraisingly even as they talked to him.

And what was his first act upon this grand playing field? This jousting court watched by the world? Failure. That was what it was: abject failure. He sat on a nearby pew and continued with his thoughts, forcing them past that first horrible moment when his ship's sails had caught the sea wind for Brittany and he had turned away from England's coast, fleeing not victory but catastrophe.

He now knew that save for that one idiot in Richard's army (he was sure there were many such but on that day and in that moment it had come down to the one), his failure would have been fatally complete. And it was in that word that he now found the courage to reconstruct his own narrative. He had failed, but not completely. His ships were lost and he himself barely made the continent on the return voyage. But barely was enough. He *had* made it back to France. He *had* survived.

Richard had not left the matter to die on the coast that day, had not been satisfied with watching his enemy flee to the continent. He had done his best to finish things, sent his best men to bribe France and Brittany with all manner of arms and money, but in the end he had failed. Richard's intense interest only confirmed what those in power on the continent now knew of a certainty, namely, that in their English guest they had a pawn at the very least, and possibly even a future king. And should he prove himself superior in the contest that was destined to play out over the next few years, well then, what better than to have a king forever in your debt? And so Henry had survived. But he had done better than merely surviving. When the dust had settled, when France and Brittany had made it clear that they understood the game and sided with him, he began to feel not so much leveraged but the master of such leverage as his unique position supplied.

He had imagined that he would arrive on the coast of England that day, fight a few battles, and then be crowned. Now he saw that the fight was not so simple, the calculation not so devoid of complexity. And then, just as he was coming to terms with himself and his situation, something good had happened. He did not at first grasp the full significance of it, but over the weeks following the October debacle, over the time when France and Brittany had mulled their roles in his fate, he had begun to see it for what it was: the beginning of the fight.

England, it seemed, was ready to stand with him. The first inkling of this came with the arrival in Brittany of a handful of English warriors and nobles. They came to pledge themselves to his cause and share his fate. But the trickle soon became a steady stream bleeding out from England's shores, and by now, at Christmastide, some three hundred or so battle-tested men stood with him. And there was more. Despite Richard's furious and vengeful wrath against him, and despite the soldiers he posted along the coast to watch for traitor's boats in the channel, messages and news continued to leak from his court as through a damaged sieve.

And so, in his narrative, the abject failure became the prelude; the real battle was yet to be fought. And on this day, in this cathedral, his captains and generals gathered with him to troth their allegiance to him and to watch him take a solemn vow. He stood, finally, and beckoned to the priest, to Jasper, and to the men beyond the shadow of light at the altar. All came forward.

The last message he had received from his mother had told him of the desire to see him betrothed to Elizabeth of York, Elizabeth Woodville's eldest daughter. Marrying the late king's daughter coupled his own claim to throne through the Beaufort's would render his right to rule impregnable.

The priest unrolled a parchment previously read and agreed to by Henry.

"Do you, Henry Tudor, Earl of Richmond, promise to take Elizabeth Woodville unto yourself as your lawful wife?"

Henry spoke loudly, his voice carrying to the back of the sanctuary, its confident tones a clarion call to action to those who stood with him.

"Aye, father, I do. And I sign here…" he paused and with a dramatic flair, inked the quill and signed his name to the contract, "… and I promise that we shall restore England to its rightful heir and to its rightful lineage, so help me God!"

The men before him knelt and the father said grace upon them all. As they rose, a call rolled forth from their ranks.

"God save the king! God save King Henry!"

For the first time in days, Henry smiled. He could now close the first part of his narrative. He had lost so that he might learn; he had fled so that he might conceive a better plan. The next time, he would die on English soil or sit upon the English throne.

Chapter Eighteen

"Do not forget, Majesty, you won."

"Aye, that I did, and without a single battle."

Richard lay upon the physician's table once more while oils mixed with herbs and astringents were applied to his bare back. The warmth was mixed with a pleasant stinging and as the masseuse began to work his magic, Richard continued the discussion with his physician.

"Tell me, sir: I have protected England from usurpation by the bastard Henry; I have provided alms aplenty and have seen that my subjects far and wide are cared for; I have bestowed crown lands upon even the most humble of those who stand with me. So tell me, what does my shoulder continue to ache? Eh? And not just continue, but to grow worse?"

The physician was an older man. Richard had moved him to London the previous summer from Middleham Castle where he had served him for over a decade. During that time, he had also become his confidante. His sure hand and steady presence gave Richard a sense of being well-cared for; he remembered the same voice, the same gentle care from the man since childhood. He trusted him.

The old man spoke now as he rattled his bottles of unguents and salves near the fire.

"You have indeed given your kingdom a marvelous year, Majesty, but it has come at some cost to yourself."

Richard liked this.

"Aye, exactly! The realm could easily have fallen into chaos last summer, but I saved it!"

He watched the physician pour himself a glass of ale and settle into a chair near the hearth.

"Yes, King Richard, but as I said, such heroic efforts for the kingdom cost you dearly. The pain in your shoulder, in your back and buttocks is nothing more than the worry, the anxiety that you carry for England manifesting itself in your physical being."

"Yes indeed." Richard lay still, allowing the massage to penetrate the ache in his shoulder.

The physician changed the subject.

"Christmas this year was most glorious, Majesty."

"Yes," Richard began to prattle happily about the size and scope of the Yuletide festivities which had just ended.

"I am told that it was the largest celebration ever for our kingdom. Of course, my coronation brought huge crowds, the largest ever I think, but this Christmas - with its food and music and fires - outshone even that precious moment."

The physician nodded contentedly. A comfortable silence interspersed with occasional gasps from Richard as the masseuse pulled his muscles and joints this way and that settled upon the room. He poured himself another ale.

"Tell me, good sir, what do you hear from the court? What rumors are abroad about me?"

The physician hesitated. It was never politic at such moments to lose control and speak the truth.

"They are grateful, Majesty, for the peace you have brought upon the land. They wish it to continue."

Richard sat up, signaling an end to the ministrations of the masseuse. Slipping on a night shirt and a robe, he dismissed the man before seating himself opposite the older man at the fire. They sat in a not-so-comfortable silence, for the physician knew Richard well. He was pensive, this evening, and that usually meant he wished to delve into his own psyche, expecting him to counter his dark thoughts with explanations which were not always easy to come by. He was not disappointed.

"So they are grateful, are they."

The physician nodded emphatically.

Richard stoked the fire.

"And the children?"

"Children, Majesty?"

"God's liver, man. Do not expect me to believe that no one speaks of my dead brother's boys."

The physician looked down. He rolled his cup carefully between his hands, only stopping when Richard made to pour him another drink.

"Yes?" the king looked at him steadily. "Do they speak of Edward? Of small Richard?"

"They do," came the slow response, "…but not often."

Richard sat. Waiting.

"And what do they say?"

Silence.

"Yes? And what…do…they…say?"

The physician sighed.

"Majesty, 'tis only a few who speak of them, I am told. No one would dare speak to me of them…"

"Why not?" Richard interjected.

The old man smiled.

"They know me to be your minister, your physician. They suspect - and rightfully so - that I would report such conversations to you forthwith."

Richard nodded and waited. Finally, the man spoke bluntly.

"They wonder, Majesty, what has become of them. They wonder if they are still alive. Should they not live still, they wonder what happened and to whom the blame should fall."

"Why blame?" Richard spoke darkly.

The physician sighed.

"Blame, Majesty, because Edward and small Richard, should they be dead, did not die of natural causes."

A great and heavy silence fell. Even the logs upon the fire seemed suspended in the moment and ceased their crackling and snapping.

"And you?" asked Richard quietly. "What do *you* think, old man?"

The physician rose and stoked the fire as he gathered his thoughts. Richard watched him warily. Finally, the man sat back down and spoke.

"Does it matter?"

For a moment Richard was confused. "Does what matter?"

"My opinion, Majesty, my thoughts upon the subject. Surely they do not, for I serve you and will continue to serve you all my days."

Richard smiled and tipped his cup slightly towards the old man.

"'Tis a good answer. You say that you will continue to serve me, even if..."

The physician raised a hand and Richard ignored him.

"...even if...you should believe they are dead."

The crackling fire alone punctuated an uncomfortable pause. Richard spoke.

"And you continue to serve me even though, should they be dead, I must surely be implicated in their deaths."

The ale in the physician's glass sloshed slightly as his hands trembled.

"King Richard, do you wish to speak something to me? Is there something affecting your health, causing your shoulder to ache constantly without letup and with such ferocious strength?"

The king merely stared into the fire in silence.

"King Richard," the physician whispered, "Should I call for a priest?"

*****

Elizabeth smiled as she read the note, and rose. A small room had been set aside in the Abbey for her and her daughters to use as a dressing room. From here, she gathered two cloaks, her own and Cecily's - she would not mind and the day was cold - and went straight away to the high rampart which overlooked London. It was from this spot that she had last seen her son, Edward V. She always spoke of him thus, even in her thoughts. It was her way of keeping hold of sanity in the face of the last few months. Edward V. King of England.

Today, however, was a good day amongst the many awful ones, and she chose to smile. The winter was a cold one this year, and she pulled the cloaks tightly about her thin frame. The Yuletide had passed within the Abbey in a quiet and empty manner. No word of her sons reached her. She was grateful for the silence and feared the day it might come to an end with fearful news of them. Today was not that day, however, and she crossed herself in wary hope. But the silence from that quarter was not her only reason to count this a joyful day. A note from another quarter had arrived, and with it, the only good tidings she had received since the October debacle had left her in tearful dread of the future.

On Christmas day, Henry had plighted his troth to her oldest daughter, Elizabeth. She pulled the note from her bosom now and reread it happily. It was done. Should the man be successful upon his next attempt to claim the English throne, her daughter would be his queen. She looked out over the city, feeling a surge of confidence for the first time in months.

Richard had usurped the crown successfully. He had taken her boys without obvious consequence, even hidden them away with impunity. But such treachery did not go unseen by heaven. The fates and angels who watched over England surely saw what he had done. How long would they wait to wreak their holy revenge upon the bastard? Today, she did not care, for she knew that it would happen. It simply could not be that a man with no morality whatsoever might be able to hold onto power for long. It was not only that heaven that would disallow it but human conscience as well.

As she looked out at the dying light of the day, she felt herself stirring to life once more. Like a butterfly from its chrysalis, she would one day soon leave sanctuary. Richard threatened and pleaded even now for her to do so. With a public contract and vow from him to leave her and her remaining children alone, she would do so, she would have to, but she would emerge stronger than before. "I am a child of God", she murmured to herself. "I am a queen of man. I shall serve the Lord all my days regardless of Richard the usurper." She realized that now he could not touch her. Her soul was beyond his grasping clutch.

Elizabeth went below to tell the girls the news of the betrothal, news that heartened her, and gave her strength, news that would continue to do so when finally they left this holy Abbey.

Before doing so, however, she made her way back to the main sanctuary. From a small box beneath a bench, she took two small candles. She placed them gently on the altar. Taking a large taper which burned nearby, she lit them slowly and reverently.

With that, she crossed herself and moved on to share this day's good news.

Chapter Nineteen

June, 1484

It was much harder than he had imagined to sell the horse.

As the sun rose on the morning following the bishop's death, Thomas had pulled to an exhausted halt on a deserted piece of commons land. He was miles from home, miles from anything in fact, in a territory he did not recognize. He had ridden north, figuring that Richard's soldiers would be concentrated in the south. But he dared not go too far, for as Agnes and the bishop had often chuckled about, his speech was that of Leicester man. To show up with a strange accent and a fabulous horse for sale would be to excite gossip, which in turn might reach the ears of those who would surely be on his trail.

He threw the great saddle and livery, sure markers of the king's property, into the brush which provided cover for him and the horse. Tethering it securely to a stout branch, he wrapped himself in the blankets from the saddle and slept fitfully till noon. The horse nudged him awake, whinnying softly for food and water. He remembered crossing a small brook a mile or so before he made camp and without speaking untied the horse and made his way there. The animal drank thirstily from the icy water as did Thomas. After a moment, he released its reins to allow it to search the nearby area for food.

What would he do now? Dressed in a priest's robes splattered with the blood of Richard's soldier, carrying the very sword which had murdered him - what hope did he have? In times of stress he would normally seek out God, ask him to show him a way through whatever trouble might be at hand. But he could not do that now, for he had murdered a man and stolen a horse. He could hardly expect the heavens to open with answers when he had stomped upon the Lord's word so thoroughly. No, he was on his own. Nor could he afford to sit and think upon a good strategy. By now, the soldier would have been missed. By now, someone would have stopped in at the bishop's manor to pass the time of day or ask for food for their table. Word was surely out, and to survive he must stay ahead of those who would find him.

He rose, patted the hungry horse and mounted it bareback. A ridge rose some miles north, and he determined to make for it. He had to find food and shelter for a cold snow was blowing in. Thomas turned into it and rode on.

A small copse grew along the western edge of the ridge, and it was here that he pulled up in the late afternoon shadows. He tied up the horse and moved forward cautiously to survey the downward slanting slope before him. Not so far away rose a haze of smoke. Aye, he could make out two, no, three chimneys: a large manor then. Perhaps he could beg food at the kitchen door. A cough behind him put an end to that line of thinking. He turned to find a man on a horse as big or bigger than the one he had just stolen.

"'Tis a fine animal you have there." A well-educated and droll baritone voice rolled quietly across the distance which separated them.

The man was on the back-side of middle-aged, with a neatly trimmed white beard and a flowing white mane to match. His cloak was of a fine wool dyed an expensive sea blue color. Upon his head was a warm knit cap over which he wore a hunter's leather one with a bright pheasant feather waving rather gaily in the snowy breeze.

Thomas bowed, trying desperately to think of an answer.

"Yeeeessss?" The man waited patiently. Thomas stood tongue-tied before him.

"Let me see. A man dressed in a priest's robes – by the by, are those bloodstains? – stands upon my ridge. Hmm. Beside him is a very fine horse, so fine, I think, that it cannot possibly be his."

The man paused and then continued on in the same dry vein.

"Wait! I see that the reins of the beast are also fine and I see that the leather straps of the bridle are embossed. Hmm."

Oh God oh God oh God. It was not a prayer as much as a salutation, for he firmly believed he was about to be dispatched to meet his maker - such was the end of all thieves and murderers. He bowed his head and waited.

But nothing happened. He looked up. The man had not moved an inch in the saddle. Thomas finally found his voice.

"Sire, all you say is true. Do what you must."

"Our good King Richard's men passed by this point not two hours ago."

Oh God oh God oh God.

"Aye. It seems they are looking for a priest and a wench who killed one of their own."

Thomas had had enough. The man was treating him like fish bait.

"Sire, did they mention that the soldier killed a bishop who had never wronged another soul in his life? Did they mention the soldier made to have the woman against her wishes and that the priest in question only acted…"

Here, Thomas broke down.

"No…I cannot say that. The priest who killed the soldier acted out of rage. Rage at the assault and murder of the old man, rage at the treatment of our Agnes - although, my instincts tell me he would have been sorry he crossed her - rage at the usurpation of the throne…"

The man did not move a muscle. Snow fell all around. Finally, he spoke again.

"Are you finished?"

"Yes, sire, and you may kill me now. I am no longer a man of God."

"Sir, might I make a suggestion?"

Thomas looked at him warily.

"You must needs get your mouth under control at once for if you do not, you will have your desire and someone will send you along to meet God very soon indeed."

"I do not understand."

"I see that." The sardonic tone returned once more to the old man's deep voice.

"You assume, o man of God (a chuckle accompanied these words), that all those about here, all those you meet support the bastard Richard and his wrongful seizure of the kingship. You assume they support the murder of our true king and his brother. You must needs rethink all that."

"Sir?" Thomas was confused.

"I stand with you sir, in your hatred of our current ruler. You did right to avenge the bishop who was murdered, and I have no idea why you believe this 'Agnes' could hold her own against the king's own man."

"She is a tough old bird, sire," Thomas began, "..and her tongue could wither an oak at ten paces."

The man on the horse grinned.

"And where is she now?"

"Safe. In Leicester."

"Aye, I understand your accent now."

He rode closer.

"Yon manor is mine. I shall employ you, oh former man of God (another chuckle), in my stables. You will do lowly work and not complain. You will muck out stalls in the winter, plow fields in the spring, and harvest my crops in the fall."

Thomas began to cry.

"God's knees, man, get a grip."

A snivel more and Thomas was done.

"I do not know what to say, sire."

"Then say nothing. Give no one cause to doubt that you are an itinerant wanderer in need of work, say nothing about what you have told me, and do not, do not under any circumstances, discuss your political thoughts and knowledge or this conversation with anyone ever. Do you hear me?"

Thomas shook his head in gratitude.

"Why do you do this for me?" he asked.

The man looked at him thoughtfully.

"For two reasons. The first is because not all men are as mean-spirited and craven as you seem to believe them to be."

"And the second?"

"I want the horse." The man smiled and shrugged his shoulders. "Now, come along. You must enter the estate with stealth and burn that garment before any about see you in it. I will give you some old clothes you may wear – they will be your own."

Thomas threw himself onto his horse's back.

"What is your name?" the old man inquired.

"Thomas."

"Well, Thomas, should the king's men make another pass through my estate, and should you not have had the wisdom to remain silent amidst my other servants, then, well, I will not be able to defend you, nor to stand with you."

"Understood, sire. Understood."

He followed the old man down a beaten track. Soon they turned onto an unused overgrown one which led to the back of the manor. Without tethering their animals, they quietly entered through a side door rusty with disuse.

"Remember my warnings, Thomas. And do not cross me."

That evening, Thomas bedded down with the horses. In all his life he had never been so weary.

Chapter Twenty

Spring, 1485

For the second time in a year, the Lyke-Wake dirge washed over him. Oh, there were other songs of mourning, of lament, but only this one moved him ever. He had insisted that it be performed, played again and again as the Christian rites of burial were carried out before him. From whence had it come, he always wondered when he heard it? Whose soul and circumstance had been so dark, whose pain had been so deep that only these simple notes could convey them; what language, he wondered, did the music speak; what would the notes say were they to open themselves up upon the page and cry forth in human tongue? He did not know.

Nor did he know why such calamity had suddenly befallen him. Him! Richard III, former Duke of Gloucester and now king of the realm! At Middleham Castle barely one year ago, as he cemented his hold on England and began to look forward to ruling rather than conquering, his only child, Edward, had died. So sudden was it that there had been no time to summon specialists or race to the bedside. Instead, he and Queen Anne, while supping late one evening, had heard first shouting and confusion, then, a whispery silence as a single knock fell upon their door. The single knock of his priest, with the news of Edward's death.

And now, one year later, Anne, too, was taken from him. He sat alone, taking part when prompted in the burial of her body. The dirge cried its tears beneath and over and all around him.

As he had moved through the days which followed her death, he had noted the sincere grief and mourning of those in his court. She had been beloved and would be missed. And all treated him with somber and quiet respect, allowing him time, so they assumed, to move past his own grief and pick up life once again. They waited for his signal.

But they were wrong. They had been wrong a year ago, and they were wrong now. It was not overpowering grief he felt, but mind-numbing fear.

And he was not a religious man - he had spent far too many years on far too many battlefields for that. He had seen death, even faced his own a time or two, and so his reaction of terror did not stem from a deep-seeded faith that drove him ever onward. Rather, his panicked anxiety arose from his lack thereof. God, it seemed, had chosen this time to make his presence known to Richard. His taking of the two souls closest to him had been a resounding clap of divine authority, an awful reminder of who truly was the ruler on high.

But it was notice as well, and Richard knew it. Notice that his past actions had not gone unseen; notice that his past transgressions against the innocent must be paid up in full; notice that evil was always checked. In the end.

He woke screaming from nightmares. He ran into the halls of his great castles demanding to know who had been in his room, who had put a pillow over his face? His physician prescribed sedatives and potions, stayed with him all night, but all to no avail: no one could stay with him in his dreams, walk through them with him. In dreamland, he was always alone. So, too, lately more and more, in his waking hours.

Over the past year, reports of the Tudor bastard had increased in number and volume. He was coming for him. Coming for his crown, for his kingdom. It had become too much and Richard had sought refuge at his home in the north, dear Middleham. Here, for two weeks, he spent his time on the ramparts as he had done so many times before. He listened to the sounds below him: the early morning opening of the draw bridge gates, the hustle and cries of the vendors, the wind as it whistled past him going its own carefree way. He walked the heather-blanketed fields and felt the wild flowers and grasses graze his fingertips. He breathed in the north, his home above all others.

He would face down the traitorous bastard who by now was more continental than English. He would best him on the battlefield. And when he was done, and Henry's head had been paraded on a spike through the streets and markets of London, then he, Richard, would turn his thoughts to God and kingdom.

"Come Henry. Come now. For when you are dispatched, I shall then become a penitent man."

Chapter Twenty-One

Summer 1485

"So it will be here, at Nottingham then?"

The men in the room - John Kendal, Robert Percy, James Tyrell - nodded slowly, thinking through the plan just presented by John Howard, Duke of Norfolk. They were northerners all, men who had ridden with Richard for a decade or more, men he knew would stand with him.

"Majesty?" Howard turned to Richard who sat at the head of the table. He had ridden there from London, calling those men whom he most trusted to the most impregnable castle in the land. He had squared himself up, and as they came to him, one by one, they recognized the Richard of old, the general who would stop at nothing to win. He had shaken off the paralysis which had seemed to grip his thoughts and his body since the death of his wife. Before them stood a decisive man of war.

Again, the question was put to him.

Nottingham Castle, Majesty? 'Tis the best place to plan and act from as needed."

Richard, too, slowly nodded.

"Yes, the cliffs of the castle provide unparalleled warning and protection. The battlements are as sound as the day they were built."

All nodded and Richard continued.

"But we will not fight here unless forced to do so, for I want a decisive victory. Here at Nottingham, our wares and horses and armor are all safe. But to fight here would give Henry the opportunity to fade away whilst we are barricaded. That is our last resort, not our first stance."

They shook their heads in agreement.

"What about the signal stations along the coast? What do we have?"

Kendal spoke.

"The stations are set, Majesty. They will be lit at first sign of Henry Tudor's fleet. From there, the signal will be picked up and carried by other stations all the way to Nottingham. We will know within moments of his being seen upon the sea."

Richard drummed his fingers restlessly on the table.

"Howard, have you commanded the nobles along the coast and inland to muster and stand ready?"

"Aye, Majesty."

Richard stood and began pacing, twisting his ring on his finger in time with his steps. Finally, the story would end.

"And no one has proved man enough to capture the bastard on foreign soil and bring him to me?"

No answer came in response. Richard stopped pacing and leaned on the table.

"'Tis already July, my lords, and we have intelligence which says he will try his luck this summer. He will find us prepared."

They bowed and left him alone. As was his habit, he poured a cup of ale and sat before the fire, twisting his ring and reviewing his plans, repeating them over and over. He would muster his forces at Nottingham Castle, but he would not fight there unless surprised. No, an open field was needed, a place where his strategies could be played out upon a grand scale, a place where Henry could be shown to be nothing, nothing at all. On an open plain, he would not be able to escape. And even should he be able to do so, through some trickery or deceit, Richard smiled, it would be for naught, for he had arranged to have Henry's ships burned as he marched inland. He would hunt him down, find him, and his end would be the same as on the battlefield.

Two hours later, having satisfied himself that indeed, the odds were with him in overwhelming number and that he had left no stone unturned in his plan for vengeance and victory, he left to join the others in the dining hall.

*****

August 1485

Those who had known the boy in exile barely recognized the man redux. The mantle of authority rested easily on his slim shoulders. The child dependent upon his Uncle Jasper, the lad who hesitated before each decision, looking to those around him for approval - these manifestations of his Henry's youth were gone. In their stead was a determined, politically-savvy man, one who understood that a second failed attempt at the crown would also be his last.

For some, the situation seemed desperate. The summer had worn on, and if they were to strike it had to be now: all the signs pointed to that necessity. They must act before the autumn storms set in, before another year solidified Richard's hold on England further still, before the unrest in the

English countryside died away, before French support for Henry's claim faded to disinterest. But those who felt that desperation did not see it mirrored in the confident operations and plans which were being laid, nor was it evident in Henry's now kingly bearing. He was a man with the wind at his back, not a foundling struggling to find a home.

*****

Thomas felt that should he stand straight, his back would snap like a twig underfoot. He was no young man when had come to the manor. He was grateful to the lord of the estate for giving him shelter in the face of his confession of murder of a king's soldier, but it had been a difficult adjustment. He worked alongside men half his age, ploughing, shoveling, hauling, trimming, repairing...whatever the manual labor needs of the estate were, his position required him to respond. He could not afford to be seen as different or as having come to this position from a different place in the world, for to do so would invite inquiry into his past. Instead, he presented himself as a wandering itinerant who just happened to fall happily into a permanent situation. Those he worked with noted his Leicester dialect and assumed that he, like so many others, had been a child too many and had been turned loose at an early age to find his own way.

There had been a storm the previous evening, and a great oak had fallen across the east field's fence line. With ten others, he had been spent the day splitting rails to set a temporary one so that no sheep might wander out. The next day they would begin removing the tree - only then could they restore the original fence. The work was monotonous, and as Thomas swung his heavy axe again and again an ache set in which seared his body from one end to the other. All day the work went on, but they were still not finished as the sun began to set.

"Leave off then," called the foreman. "We will finish tomorrow."

A collective sigh rose from the group of sweaty men as they ceased and wiped their brows.

"We will make better time should we have a supply to begin with in the morn," the man continued. "Will anyone stay and work on until the light is completely gone?"

A laugh arose: all studiously avoided eye contact, looking off into the distance or down at the ground as though riveted by what they saw. After a moment, Thomas raised his hand.

"Aye, I will see to a supply for the morrow," he chuckled. "These young bucks cannot keep up with a man twice their age."

His light tone hid the fatigue that consumed him, but as always, he felt he must go the extra distance lest his position be questioned.

The foreman looked around for others.

"And none of the rest of you?"

Again, no volunteers.

"Then, old man, only you shall have dinner in the kitchen tonight when you are done. You will eat all you can and afterwards, I will see to a hot bath for you."

Other hands immediately shot up and voices clamored in the fading light. The foreman laughed.

"Too late! Get your tools and get on!"

As the grumbling died away and they began their slow walk back to the barns and stables where they quartered, the foreman nodded to Thomas.

"Use care, old man. And do not work when the light is too gone - I cannot afford to lose a fine worker like yourself."

Thomas smiled and nodded at the compliment. It was almost worth the pain he felt as he picked up his axe and turned again to his work.

*****

"Aye, are you the man who continued on?" asked the old woman who answered the bell at the kitchen door.

"Aye." Thomas was too tired to say more. He had worked hard and fast to assemble a sizeable stack of posts for the morrow's work, continuing on right up until the final ray from the summer sun had slid beneath the horizon. The foreman would be pleased. A slight breeze carrying the scent of summer refreshed him as he walked slowly across the pasture and back to the manor house. There was fresh grass in its breath, and the scent of wild lavender and apples were left behind as it moved on.

When the woman opened the door, the smells of a busy kitchen rushed out to meet him. She eyed him critically as he stepped in.

"You will want that bath first, aye, you will." It was a command, not a statement.

"Liza," she yelled over her shoulder, "Is that water ready?"

A young woman came tripping to her side. She was not fair, but handsome. Her hair was chestnut, tied up in a bright kerchief, and while her apron showed signs of current use, the frock beneath was clean. She looked shyly at Thomas and curtsied.

"Enough of that. This man is here for a bath and a meal, not a welcome fit for kings."

The woman blushed and nodded.

"You," the old woman pointed a finger at him, "You will use the tub set just beyond that screen, and do not," here her voice became rough, "Do NOT think to show yourself in any form of undress in my kitchen. Are we clear?"

She was an older Agnes, Thomas thought, and as he was led to the screened area, he wondered what had happened to her. She had many friends in the village, and he hoped she had found a home.

"And give me your clothes."

The old woman continued to bark at him, at the scullery maids, at anyone it seemed who crossed her path. He passed the clothes to her and she made a noise like a retching as she took them.

"God's knees, man, you are a filthy one."

He heard her moving away, still barking.

"Jess, you are his size. Go and get a set of clean clothes for our visitor."

"*My* clothes?" came the indignant response from a man Thomas could only assume was Jess. "Why mine?"

"Aye, you heard me. And put these with the washing for the morrow. He will borrow yours and return them when his are clean."

"I never..." Jess' voice trailed away and Thomas eased himself into the tub filled with hot water.

"And no splashing onto my floor! Do you hear me?"

Thomas would not have dreamed of wasting a single drop of the steamy heaven-sent liquid which was his reward. His felt his back began to loosen and he ducked his head beneath the warm waves again and again. Aye, he would have swung his axe a thousand times more for such a treat. The grime of a great many months floated away, and his muscles responded to the heat by ceasing their aches and pains. He rested his head on the back of the tub and was almost asleep when a sharp rap on the top of the screen brought him round.

"Get out of the tub! What do you think this is? Eh? An inn? A paradise where I wait upon you like some king?"

The old woman cackled in appreciation of her own joke, and threw Jess's clothes over the screen.

"Either you are at the table forthwith, or I shall be forced to feed your meal to the pigs."

Thomas stepped lightly and was around the screen within seconds. The young woman and the old one too both smiled broadly, for the food upon the long table was clearly not meant for swine.

"The foreman said to feed you up right."

Thomas feasted on ham, on bread and cheese, on lamb and more bread and ale, ale and ale. House servants floated in and out, sitting at the long table beside him and across from him, ignoring the man who ate like he had never seen food before as they ate their evening supper. Thomas listened to their chatter with only mild interest. It was nothing to him what the Lady Bess thought of this or that, or what the Lord John wanted to do tomorrow. He did not care about the latest fashions. He was therefore only half listening when the young lord's valet spoke of their trip to town from which they had only just returned.

"Oh, aye, I would like to have gone with you," remarked a houseman. "Did you stay at the Blue Boar Inn?"

No one noticed the stranger pause as he reached for yet another piece of lamb.

"Aye, we did. 'Tis a fine place. Have you stayed there with the Master Peter?"

The houseboy shook his head.

"No, when we go to Leicester, we stay with the lord's aunt."

Thomas continued eating slowly, listening now to every word. He had heard nothing of Leicester since his night escape.

The houseboy poured them both more ale and asked, "And what do you hear of King Richard, um?"

Thomas almost stopped breathing.

The valet lowered his voice before answering.

"Oh, that man, evil he is and 'tis evil that's befallen him. You know his son and his wife died."

"No! When?"

The valet nodded.

"Queen Anne passed just this year, but that is not the news which makes its way across Leicester."

The houseboy leaned forward, eyes big.

"It seems," Thomas strained to hear the whispered words, "...it seems that Henry Tudor is here."

"What? In *England*?"

The valet nodded.

"Aye, he has come to wrest the throne away from that wicked man and restore it to Edward V."

"But," came the hesitant response, "Everyone knows that Richard murdered Edward."

"Then Henry shall sit upon the throne himself. And he will not be a usurper, for 'tis said he is betrothed to poor little Edward's sister, the Lady Elizabeth."

The valet paused, then added.

"They say Richard is garrisoned at Nottingham Castle, barricaded behind its cliffs."

"Nottingham? 'Tis no distance from here!"

"Aye."

They sat in silence, digesting the news.

"What will happen? Where is Henry Tudor? How will he take the throne?"

The valet shrugged.

"No one knows, for it is said that his only army is one of French convicts. He must hope – we all must hope – that he picks up support as he marches to do battle with Richard. 'Tis his only chance. And ours as well."

The conversation drifted to other things.

*****

So Richard would be taken down. Thomas left the kitchen and spat as he thought of the man. It was he who had stolen the throne and murdered two children to do so. It was he who had brought his soldier to Leicester and he whom Thomas held responsible for his own circumstance and for the death of Bishop Jonson. Over time, he believed he had come to terms with that night. His feelings tonight upon hearing the news told him he had not. He had simply buried his rage beneath the necessity of eking out a living. Now, as it roiled to the surface, he could not think.

There was a man - Henry Tudor - who would stand up to Richard. Thomas saw it clearly as a mighty war between good and evil. In one go he might could avenge the bishop's death and take action against the one who had destroyed his own life.

But where would this battle occur? Had it already happened?

He leaned against the side of the barn, thinking hard. How could he get news?

Suddenly, a smile crossed his weathered face. He no longer felt tired.

With a stealth born of necessity, Thomas walked on and slipped unseen into the stable where the lord of the manor's horses were kept. The house might still be awake but those who labored for their living were dead to the world already. He walked along the stalls, seeking one he knew well. A gentle nuzzle told him he was there.

"Aye, boy, 'tis me," Thomas murmured to the great beast. "Remember our ride together?"

The animal seemed to respond by shaking its head. Thomas smiled.

"We shall do it again, friend."

The horse snorted.

"Wait."

He moved quietly out of the stable and ran quickly to his own stall in a far barn. There, he reached beneath his straw mattress and pulled the sword which he had hidden away there on his first night.

Moving back to the stable, he located a full set of tack on the wall. With the saddle and bridle in one hand and the sword in his belt, he returned to the stall and slowly slid the door open.

"Aye, we shall ride again." Thomas spoke softly as he saddled the animal and fed the bridle over its ears.

"Our liege will not mind, I am certain."

The horse pawed the hay.

Thomas smiled and led it outside. Taking a path seldom trodden, he made his way to the ridge where once before he and the great destrier had paused. With a final look behind him, he turned and galloped into the night.

*****

A small rap on the door woke her and she looked around, confused. The rap came again. Straightening her night cap and pulling a blanket round her she moved across the small cell she called her own and opened the door. The priest who stood there held the lit nub of a candle. Before she could speak, he put his finger to his lips and led her down the stairs to the small sitting room they shared. The fire was almost out in the hearth and only illuminated the shadow of the man standing there. She looked at the priest questioningly: was this some hungry soul in need of a meal? If so, could not he wait until the dawn and breakfast? As if in answer to her unspoken questions, the man turned.

"Agnes."

She squinted and peered.

"So Thomas, you could not wait until dawn?"

He shook his head.

"Aye, I could not, for I am here on urgent business."

"Well, it cannot be so urgent that I cannot dress properly and make us all something hot."

The priest nodded.

"I shall stir the fire. Sit stranger, and take your leave."

*****

As dawn broke over Leicester, Thomas slept in the priest's room. Agnes had long since stabled the horse at the inn next door.

At noon, she woke him and they sat for a final meal before the fire.

"And you are sure of this intelligence?" he asked.

Both she and the priest nodded.

"Aye," she confirmed. "Henry Tudor comes up from the south even now. Richard has begun his move towards Leicester from Nottingham Castle."

"And you do not believe they will battle here in the town?"

The priest shook his head.

"I have it on good authority that Richard intends to engage him just south of here. He will use Leicester as his base, but he wants to catch Henry on an open plain."

"But south of here are the bogs and fens," Thomas said, puzzled.

Agnes shrugged.

"We can only tell you what we hear."

Thomas nodded and stood.

"Then I shall ride that way until I meet Henry. He shall have my services."

"Thomas," asked the priest, "Would you like communion before you go?"

A stricken look crossed Thomas' face.

"No father, for I am outside the church now."

"Then you will have our prayers."

Agnes led him to the stable next door where his horse waited. She pointed to two leather pouches attached to the saddle.

"'Tis food and ale for you."

They looked at one another. Thomas was about to hug her when she made a disgusted sound.

"Oh, nay, there will be none of that. You know me better."

Thomas smiled as he swung himself into the saddle.

"As sentimental as ever, Agnes."

"Get on, old man, and may God speed."

Chapter Twenty-Two

Agnes' intelligence proved right as usual.

As the sun settled over the horizon on August 7, 1485, Henry's small fleet nosed its way into Milford Haven, a port in the county of Pembroke. They had been prepared to fight their way ashore, but the scene was strangely deserted. There were no soldiers threatening them from the shore and no banners peeked from behind the craggy hills of the bay.

"Is it possible?" muttered Jasper. "Do they not have signal fires? Did they not see us coming?"

Henry shook his head.

"No. I mean aye, they have them, but Richard wants a decisive battle. He does not want me killed by some insignificant local noble before I am barely on English soil. He wants the honor himself."

Henry stepped from the dory and onto English soil for the first time since he and Jasper fled in 1471. He knelt and kissed the sand. As he rose, he searched the hills and shoreline in the dying light.

"He waits for us, Jasper."

His uncle slapped him on the back.

"Well then, let us not keep the 'king' waiting too long."

The next morning, 2,000 French convicts marched out behind Henry's banner.

*****

Henry was overwhelmed, caught in a wash of strategies and memories. He had reckoned, *counted* on, picking up local support as he marched to meet Richard but he had not counted on the visceral sense of déjà vu which settled over him and which he could not seem to shake. It was still there the next morning as they rode into Haverfordwest and the town pledged its allegiance to him - in English and in Welsh. He had to listen intently to the words, to watch the body language of the speakers as they spoke in order to ensure a complete understanding. He was accustomed to the rhythm of Jasper's English, which was overlain with the cadence and nuances of fourteen years of French. This language which he now heard, in shouted chorus and in the ritual welcoming by the mayor, fell tinny upon his ear. And yet he recognized it. Something deep stirred within him, and snatches of his life before exile began flashing through his mind.

He had anticipated resistance but found instead gates thrown wide everywhere in welcome to him. He had believed it would be necessary to fight and conquer in order to inspire loyalty. It had come as a complete surprise, then, when he realized that all he really needed was what he had been all along: a son of Wales, a man of honor, an heir to a throne which had been usurped. Armed with those powerful intangibles, he rode forward.

The plan had always been simple. They would march north or east or west - wherever Richard awaited them. They would engage him in decisive battle, a battle to which there would be only two possible outcomes. Henry relished that - the binary nature of the end game. It helped keep the everyday clutter of an army on the move, generals jockeying for position, the strangeness of home and the desperate need for support in graphic perspective.

So they rode. Day after day, town after town. And as they did, the strangest thing of all began to happen. A trickle of recruits became a steady stream, became a river, became a flood. Word went out through the land that he was coming, that those who wanted to stand against Richard finally had a champion. Through Cardigan and Aberystwyth, turning eastward and catching fire in the Vale of Powys he rode on. There was a moment of consternation when a black banner, that of Rhys ap Thomas, appeared. But he, too, pledged to Henry.

Time passed rapidly as events oscillated between the mundane (whoever made the breakfast must never do so again) to the sublime (did that rainbow portend victory?). Finally, news of Richard no longer needed to be brought from afar with weeks of waiting and suspense between reports. Now, there was almost no time to siphon through it all, so close were the two armies. His scouts routinely made the trip to Nottingham and back to Henry in one day.

As they broke for camp on the evening of the 18th, southwest of the town of Leicester, Jasper and Henry rode out together to reconnoiter what lay ahead.

"So he moves from Nottingham Castle, now," Jasper said quietly. Their horses walked side by side in the late afternoon son. Its rays danced and shimmered on the nearby fields. Past those a marshy area came into view.

"Aye," Henry spoke and then pointed. "Those, then, are the fens?"

Jasper nodded.

"'Tis a bog and when it rains, it becomes impassible."

"What do our scouts say of the territory? Where will we have the advantage?"

Jasper kicked his mount to a gallop and drove him up a small knoll which gave a view of the surrounding countryside as Henry followed suit. In the distance lay Leicester.

"Here," Jasper pointed northeast of their present position.

"Aye," Henry murmured. "'Tis large enough to maneuver. Do we have a new estimate of his numbers?"

"Ten thousand."

Henry whistled.

"To our five thousand."

Jasper pointed across the plain.

"That road yonder is known as Watling Street."

"The highway to London," Henry rejoined and Jasper confirmed with a nod.

"And that rise - there…" he pointed again, "…do you see the cluster of buildings? That is Sutton Cheney. Richard will use that as his muster point."

"Aye."

After a while, they turned and rode back to camp. Henry tumbled the odds about in his mind.

It was possible, but not without a fair portion of help from above.

Chapter Twenty-Three

August 20, 1485

He left Nottingham Castle with the crown upon his head.

"Let no man suffer from the illusion that Henry will be kind or merciful should he wear this crown," he called out as he rode before his men. "As he would do unto us, so too must we resolve to do to him. We win or we die."

A great cheer went up and they closed ranks behind him. The pennant bearers rode before him, his army behind.

There was no question of his route, nor did he harbor doubts about where he would finally meet Henry Tudor. He made for Leicester, reaching the city's north gate by late afternoon. Waiting for him there were Henry Percy, the Earl of Northumberland, and his most trusted lieutenant John Howard, Duke of Norfolk. Leaving their armies behind, they rode on, clattering across the West Bridge and riding on to Sutton Cheney. Three thousand of Norfolk's archers had secured the ridge, and busied themselves polishing their longbows. The six-foot long weapons of yew had a reach of two hundred and fifty yards or more. Tudor may have wanted the high ground, but they would deny him that. Richard took in the lay of the terrain before him. Like a thousand battles before, he plotted his moves in his mind, each one an individual maneuver orchestrated towards one final chorus of victory for him, humiliation for his enemy. Henry would ride up from the south past the fens, with nothing but a vast and empty field before him. Richard smiled - he had the advantage in numbers, in high ground, and in knowledge of the area. Yes, he would win. He always did.

By nightfall, there was nothing more to be done. The campfires of Henry Tudor's men glowed against the night sky and the three men turned back towards their own encampment. Passing along the line, Richard's confidence began to swell. The clanking of armor being readied was a familiar and steeling noise to him. Each man would carry a variety of weapons, from swords to picks to halberds. Upon news of his coming, each man rose and stood silent vigil as he passed. They, too, were ready.

That evening, he chose solitude, leaving his generals to their own devices. For the first time in months, his shoulder did not ache.

Chapter Twenty-Four

August 22, 1485

Bosworth Field

Thomas woke early from a fitful sleep. He had long since ceased marveling at the circumstances in which he now found himself. His work as a scholar seemed as distant in time as the manuscripts he had once studied.

He had thought the ride from Leicester would be difficult and he kept his long-sword at the ready. But the road south was choked with men on the same journey. Some had armor and banners, others had longbows, still others an assortment of ancient and modern weapons; there were those on foot, those on mule and those on plough horses or warhorses. But common purpose defied class and rank and provided a strange unity even amongst the classes. A camaraderie, a hopeful spirit borne of the possibility of a new day, rode with them.

Thomas shared his food and his horse with those around him. Should one tire, he rode. Should another go lame, he rode. Relationships which normally took a lifetime to build were cemented in a matter of days along the dusty roads leading to Henry's army. Thomas and his small coterie met Henry's advance forces as they left the marches of Wales and crossed the great plain towards Leicester. Their common goal was the defeat of Richard, but Thomas' plans went further. The men around him seemed content with the vision of a Richard-less throne; Thomas wanted more. It was not enough to slay Richard - everything depended upon Henry surviving the battle. Should Richard die at the hands of Henry's army and Henry be slain as well, their cause was lost, for civil war would surely ensue, once again ripping England apart. And should Henry lose, it was imperative that he live to fight another day - besides him, there were only pretenders to the throne.

Henry's main army came on, and the exodus of men from Leicester was slowly rolled up within it. Thomas rode further back, seeking Henry himself. Seeing him at a distance, surrounded by those who had become his elite guard, with him since France - he slowed, keeping the man at a distance yet close enough so that he, Thomas, might protect him should the need arise. It was in this manner that they made camp on August 21st. But while others gathered in small knots, cleaning their weapons and sharing their histories, Thomas sat alone, intent on salvation and revenge.

"You there."

The words cut into his personal reverie as he polished his long-sword. Looking up, he saw a man he had seen previously next to Henry.

"I say, what unit are you with? Under what knight's banner do you serve?"

Thomas stood before answering.

"I serve Henry Tudor."

The man's eyes narrowed as he glanced at Thomas' sole, antiquated weapon.

"And how do you intend to do that?"

"By protecting him."

The general would have laughed save for the serious mien of Thomas.

"And armor? You have armor?"

"No."

"So, Sir I-have-no-armor-and-only-a-long-sword," the general smiled kindly, impressed by the rawness of the man before him, "You would save Henry Tudor with…"

Thomas interrupted him.

"Forgive me, sire, but I would not save Henry Tudor. I would save our sovereign, King Henry."

The general bowed slightly.

"But you have no armor. Do you have a horse?"

Thomas laughed.

"Aye, a fine one just there." He pointed to the impossibly large horse some distance from him, eating hay peacefully. The general raised an eyebrow.

"Stolen, sir."

"From?" came the surprised response.

"From Richard. He rides tomorrow with one less soldier."

The general laughed at the brazen contempt of the man's words.

"Your name?"

"Thomas, sire. And note that the horse was stolen with no armor, only a long-sword."

He laughed again at the sheer audacity.

"Well, ride close with us tomorrow, Thomas, for even a long-sword is a weapon and we shall need all the bravery we can get our hands upon."

Thomas bowed silently as the man moved on, pausing and speaking to others as he went.

Indeed, he thought as he watched him go, I shall stay close.

*****

They marched with the sun in their faces, their enemy on the high ridge before them. From his vantage point in Sutton Cheney, Richard watched them coming, rolling across the plain like a great wave.

"They do not split up into separate units," he observed to Norfolk.

"Aye. Likely they worry that the maneuver would lead to isolated pockets which could then be surrounded, and taken out one by one."

"Will they hold, do you think, when our archers are finished and we take the field?"

Norfolk laughed.

"That rabble? French convicts, indentured men, village souls with no weapons to speak of?"

He paused.

"No, they will not hold. They will be slaughtered shortly."

He turned as the first hail of arrows from Henry's archers sprinkled the ranks of their own.

"NOW!" he bellowed. The trumpet blared. The battle had begun.

*****

But the ranks of Henry's army held the line. They had been ordered not to stray from their respective lords, each identified with his signature pennant. And each lord, in turn, kept a watchful eye upon his men, lest any chose to try and defy the order. Wave after wave of Richard's well-equipped soldiers were repulsed or pulled into hand to hand combat by a wall of Henry's men.

Henry watched warily from behind the front lines.

"We do well, do we not?"

He spoke to the soldier nearest him. Jasper and the other veterans had ridden forward. Henry was no fool - he had no experience of battle. His choice was either to ride into the fray and possibly be killed, or to let his competent generals marshal his men. He made the wise decision. Richard, too, stayed back upon the ridge, becoming increasingly restless as the hand to hand mauling grew worse, each side slogging it out in murderous fashion.

"Norfolk," he called. "Tell Stanley to let loose his men." He referred to Sir William Stanley, one who had promised Richard allegiance but whose troops still sat, unengaged, on the far west side of the field.

Norfolk coughed and Richard looked at him sharply.

"Do as I say."

"It has been done already, Majesty."

"Then why does the good Stanley still sit upon his arse while we carry the brunt of the fighting? He is needed *now*, while we still have the advantage. The bastard is beginning to gain momentum as his line holds our attack. Break it now!"

Norfolk shouted at him over the whine of arrows and the sound of clashing metal on the field beneath them.

"He has declined, sire."

Richard stared at him in disbelief.

"What?" he shouted.

"Declined!"

An unholy fury was written across Richard's face, but it was an impotent one. He would have to settle with Stanley latter. At this moment he must find a way to deal with the increasingly uncomfortable situation playing out below. Henry could not easily win against his sizeable army, but if his generals continued to prove competent enough to avoid defeat, it might be as good as a victory in the end. Richard needed to beat him decisively here and now, this day, with no possibility of a tomorrow. Suddenly a distant banner, larger than the others on the plain, caught his attention. Shielding his eyes with his hand, he shouted at Norfolk.

"Look yonder!"

Norfolk squinted and followed Richard's finger. He grinned as he turned in his saddle.

"'Tis Henry himself. How thoughtful of him to mark his position with that gaudy red dragon."

Richard suddenly smiled.

"I know how we shall defeat the bastard." His words were barely audible above the noise and chaos.

Norfolk waited for him to continue.

"I shall take my personal guard and outflank his center."

Norfolk nodded, understanding Richard's intent.

"If you rode like the wind, Majesty, you might reach him before his generals have time to react."

Richard nodded.

"How many are with him? Can you see?"

Norfolk again squinted and looked long.

"They do not number more than your guard. Even odds at best."

It was all Richard needed. Minutes later, his guard left the ridge and galloped madly round the far edge of the plain. They were past the melee in a mere minute. Behind them rode Richard, his sword drawn, his face a mask of rage.

Thomas had as yet not engaged. He kept apart, finding it helped him focus on the larger picture rather than the individual battles taking place before him. Suddenly, he noticed a small portion of the line upon the enemy ridge begin to move. With no hesitation, they began a headlong rush down the eastern portion of the farther slope. They picked up speed and to Thomas' horror neatly flanked the main battle line. There was precious little between them and Henry and they rode like demons from hell on a Hallow's Eve.

But Thomas was not the only one with a sharp eye. Jasper, too, saw what was happening. He shouted to those nearest him and turned back towards Henry. His order was caught up in turn by a knight on horseback whose contingent had been kept in reserve. He turned his men to face Richard's guard.

Henry drew his sword and prepared to ride forward with them.

"NO!" came Thomas' urgent scream. "Stay here, Majesty!"

Henry hesitated.

"Do it!" Thomas dispensed with protocol and Henry obeyed.

The knight's men were holding Richard's guard and Jasper was coming up from behind yelling furiously.

"Hold the line! Hold the line!"

Thomas positioned himself in front of Henry. As he did so, a single soldier from Richard's guard broke free and thundered towards him. Richard rode behind, his face maniacal, mirroring his intent. In the seconds before he was upon them, Thomas jerked his reins with all his might, causing his horse to turn broadside into the onrushing horse's path. With a shout of victory, he ducked the swing of the man's short sword and swung his own in a high and powerful arc.

The searing slash pierced the man's armor at his neck. But the momentum of the swing and the impact of the other rider had thrown Thomas' mount off center. With a terrified whinny, it fell on the side nearest Henry, trapping Thomas beneath. Though he wrestled to free himself, he could not. For the first time, Thomas met the gaze of the man who would be his sovereign.

"Long live King Henry!" he shouted to his on-looking sovereign.

Then he disappeared in muck beneath the destrier.

Richard galloped up mere seconds later, sword at the ready. But Jasper's timely arrival forestalled him. Attacking from behind, he forced Richard's horse to turn before he could reach Henry. The ground was soft, too soft, and his horse began to struggle, unable to move beyond its straightened circumstance. Richard found himself alone and surrounded. The battle on the plain raged on, the give and take of the line ebbing and flowing like a living, breathing organism. The archers continued their assault from on high while down below horses neighed in terror, men screamed in pain, but all meant nothing save one thing alone. In the fens of Bosworth Field, Richard fell.

*****

"Long live King Henry!"

The shout rose and echoed up and down the ridge as both armies realized that Richard was dead. William Stanley, late to the game but nevertheless having fought on Henry's side, found among the battlefield relics the crown Richard had worn into battle.

With ceremony and purpose, he knelt before Henry and rising, situated the muddy diadem upon his head.

Long live King Henry.

Chapter Twenty-Five

Sunday, October 30, 1485

Elizabeth Woodville made her way alone to the narrow walkway around the massive roof of the Abbey's main cathedral. The wind was blowing cold – it would be a hard winter. There were crowds on the street below, and she watched with them as Henry Tudor entered the Abbey for his coronation.

Elizabeth, her daughter would marry Henry in December; her husband's legacy, at least, was safe; and the kingdom was at peace. She took in the scene before her, then walked slowly back to the small nave she called her own. With a solemnity borne of a thousand tears, she lit two small candles upon the altar. A gentleness settled over her and she stood for sometime, watching them flicker and burn.

Without a word, she turned and followed the music to the main cathedral below.

Chapter Twenty-Six

Spring 1486

Greenwich Palace

Henry stopped almost mid-gallop.

"Halt! Stop!"

A stable boy with the leads of two destriers in his hands paused, bowing deeply.

"What is it?" asked Henry's companion.

"That horse. I know it."

Henry turned to the stable boy.

"Where did you get this horse?" he motioned toward the huge, ebony one nearest him.

The boy trembled.

"Come, lad. You are not accused of anything. Answer me."

"I believe it was one of the horses which came to us after Bosworth, Majesty. There were many such animals and we have parceled them out to various of your palaces so that you might ride them at your pleasure."

They rode closer and Henry dismounted, inspecting the mighty beast. His friend spoke from his saddle.

"Aye, I know that horse as well."

Henry turned to him intently as he continued to speak.

"It was indeed at Bosworth, Majesty. Its owner saved your life."

Henry grew excited.

"Yes! The man with no armor! He threw himself fearlessly before Richard's guard. We would not be here now had he not done so."

The friend nodded somberly.

"I wish I knew him, for I would give him a proper reward," Henry said solemnly. "Was he killed when the horse fell upon him?"

His friend shrugged.

"Likely." Pause. "I met him, you know, the day before the great battle."

Henry listened.

"He was camped near you but on his own. I am sad to say I laughed at the man's long sword and lack of armor."

"What did he say?"

"He ignored my jibe and told me he would protect you. And when I asked him how he would protect Henry Tudor, he interrupted me."

"Go on!"

"He corrected me, Majesty, and said that he was not protecting Henry Tudor, but Henry, King of England."

Henry began pacing.

"I should find this man. I have rewarded all, great and small, and yet this one who truly saved my kingdom and my life goes without. Did he say anything about his origins? His liege?"

The friend shook his head.

"No, but he was an educated man, for he spoke quite well."

He thought harder.

"And his dialect. Yes, I am certain: he was from Leicester. He had likely ridden out with the others to meet your army and fight on your behalf."

Now he laughed.

"Yes! I remember now! I asked him where he got such a magnificent animal, and he calmly told me that he had stolen it from one of Richard's soldiers."

Henry's eyes lit up.

"Educated and from a small town. Go now and find this man. Bring him to me."

"As you say, sire, but he may be dead."

"Then find his family for me. Living or dead, he will not go unrewarded."

The friend turned and left at once, as though his life depended upon pleasing the new king. But it did not and he knew it did not. He and the rest of England simply found joy at finally having a lasting peace in the realm and a rightful sovereign to rule it.

As he sat at repast much later, Jasper joined him.

"How was the hunt today, King Henry?"

Henry laughed.

"You, and you alone, may call me Henry."

"I know."

Jasper pauses.

"As I asked, how was the hunt today, *King* Henry?"

Henry smiled.

"Greenwich Wood is well stocked. It will be my ongoing pleasure to reduce its stags by a goodly number."

They ate in silence.

"Tell me," Henry said, "…on the far side of the wood is a small meadow which abuts a rather sudden ridge."

Jasper nodded.

"Yes, I have seen it when I hunted on my own here last week. And on the further side of the ridge is a very small abandoned manor house."

"Is it upon crown land? The last thing I need is another palace or castle."

"Yes, I believe so. I stopped there and went in to see what its condition was."

"And?"

"Very medieval. It was a monastery at one point, from the looks of it, later converted to a lodge for some king's use."

Henry nodded.

"I tell you this," Jasper said as he helped himself to more venison, "…'tis charming. There are the ruins of a small chapel to one side, and the manor house itself is richly furnished with fine rugs and tapestries. And the beginnings of a fine collection of manuscripts. 'Tis a pity it will go to ruin."

They finished their meal and played cards until midnight.

Chapter Twenty-Seven

Summer 1486

Greenwich Palace

"I have found him."

"Who?"

"The man with no armor."

Henry jumped off from his throne and pulled the man into a private room, away from the public glare of his courtiers.

He looked expectantly at him.

"He awaits you now."

"Where?"

The man nodded.

"In the small dining room. But I warn you, Majesty, he is not happy to be here."

Henry waited.

"It took some time for anyone in Leicester to give him up. He has a story. He defended a beloved bishop against a soldier of Richard's. Killed him in fact. In fear of what would happen, he stole the soldier's horse and fled the region. Only upon hearing of your arrival on English soil did he come forward so as to fight for you."

Henry stroked his chin.

"What kind of man was he?"

"He was a priest by training, but a scholar by nature. Apparently, he and the old bishop collected manuscripts and spent their days studying the dusty old relics."

"Manuscripts?"

"Aye," his said quizzically.

Henry clapped him on the back.

"That will be all. Tell my valet I will be riding shortly with a friend. I will need two horses."

The friend smiled.

"The Bosworth beast?"

Henry smiled and walked on.

*****

You are Thomas, my friend tells me."

Thomas bowed deeply and nodded warily.

Henry noticed the man's leg.

"Is that from when the horse fell on you?"

"Aye, your Majesty," came the wary reply.

"Can you still ride?"

"'Tis difficult and painful, Sire."

Henry looked at him with a playful smile.

"Can you ride one more time, Thomas? I wish you to accompany me through Greenwich Wood. There is something I wish to show you."

Thomas did not answer.

"Sire, I am confused…" he began.

Henry waved his hand.

"All will be clear soon enough. Sit, have some ale, and I will join you shortly."

*****

Henry had arranged weeks ago for the brambles which covered the gates to be cut back. They approached them now and Henry turned to his guard.

"You two will stay. You two will come and assist my friend with his dismount."

He turned and rode to Thomas.

"Coudenoure," he motioned at the word carved in grand letters in the gate post.

"I have no idea what it means."

Thomas smiled.

"Nor I, Majesty. Did you wish to show me something?"

They continued up the rutted, overgrown drive of the place.

"'Tis lovely, is it not? A pity it has gone to seed."

"Aye," Henry said complacently. "And there are manuscripts in its small library which lay unstudied. Untouched."

Silence ensued save for the clop of the horses' hooves.

"And the church ruins? Still lovely, do you not agree?"

"They add character," Thomas said simply.

Even with assistance, it had been difficult for him to dismount and the pain showed on Thomas' face.

"We are almost there," declared Henry.

One of the guards opened wide the ancient wych elm doors and Henry took Thomas' elbow, guiding him to the great room just off the hallway which ran the length of the house. He opened the doors to a room with a large hearth, a crackling fire, and two footmen standing ready.

"What is this?" Thomas asked.

"'Tis your new home, Thomas. England is forever indebted to you, and I pay her bills."

Thomas laughed.

"Majesty, I am a defrocked priest with a lame leg. I cannot afford that stick of furniture there, much less this place or its upkeep."

"I have thought of that," Henry smiled. "It comes with a small stipend for the crown. Oh, it will not be easy to pull it back from disaster, but the effort will be good for you."

Thomas stood unmoving.

"Come, sit. You must tell me of this bishop of yours."

And they began from there.

#####

[To be continued by Rise of the Tudors 2. Follow the saga of Thomas de Grey's family in the Royal Sagas series; four volumes presently available: "The Seventh Wife of Henry VIII", "The Other Elizabeth", "King James' Aversion", and "Kingdom's End" by Betty Younis.]

Made in the USA
Coppell, TX
21 July 2020

31367727R00142